# Eternal Flame

# Eternal Flame

Jean  8/09

Thanks for keeping Elvis' memory so bright!
Blessings

*Patricia Garber*

Copyright © 2007 by Patricia Garber.

Library of Congress Control Number: 2007902676
ISBN:     Hardcover     978-1-4257-6774-7
          Softcover     978-1-4257-6768-6

All rights reserved. No part of this book may be reproduced or transmitted in any form or by any means, electronic or mechanical, including photocopying, recording, or by any information storage and retrieval system, without permission in writing from the copyright owner.

This is a work of fiction. The characters are all either fictious or used in a fictious manner. Names, incidents and places are combined with the authors imagination for entertainment only.

This book is not authorized or endorsed by the Estate of Elvis Presley or by the estate of any other person.

This book was printed in the United States of America.

To order additional copies of this book, contact:
Xlibris Corporation
1-888-795-4274
www.Xlibris.com
Orders@Xlibris.com
37175

## *Dedication*

For my mother, who is the strongest woman
I will ever know. I love you.

# ACKNOWLEDGEMENTS

I want to send out thanks to Cindy Lundeen, my editor and friend. Without your talent for words and help through this process, I would have been truly lost. I owe you a big thanks topped with heaps of love! And yes, "heaps" is a word, but am I using it right? Now that is the question.

Thank you also to all my friends—too many to list, but you know who you are. To have one true friend in your corner of life makes a person a lucky individual; to have many is to be truly blessed! I count myself fortunate to call all of you my dearest friends.

Big thanks to my large Italian family. You all have taught me what family really means. In your support and love, I have found a resting place I call home. I wouldn't trade you for anything in the world. That is, unless anyone has homemade bread? Just kidding!

To my mom, who raised me alone in the midst of life's struggles and taught me by example how to love. You are my hero. I've watched you forgive with your entire soul, with a giving and caring heart, no matter the circumstance. With God's help, I hope to be just like you one day.

A special thanks goes to my husband, Marc. You are the one man who has stood by me, loving me always. It's because of you that I have renewed hope for all that is mankind. We are the greatest team God ever allowed to come together. I love you, baby!

Thank you to the fans of Elvis Presley, the most beloved entertainer in the world. I have traveled all over, meeting you and befriending you. I'm honored to call myself an Elvis fan. Thanks to our shared love for this special man, a fantasy made its way to paper. A story, in part, I've been carrying around with me since his untimely passing. It's my hope that I give you all many hours of entertainment and as much joy in reading it as I had in creating it. For a while, lets just pretend he didn't go.

Most importantly, thanks be to God! He is the reason for my very being and the one to whom I happily give all praise. You're so very patient with "your" work in progress. You are the true "KING."

# CHAPTER 1

*Dear Diary, it's been a long time since we last spoke. I need help, and I don't know where to turn anymore. I have made some bad choices in my life so far, but the mess I've managed to get into this time tops them all. What does a girl do when she falls in love with something that doesn't belong to her? She knows this cannot go on, but the idea of living without it seems worse than the repercussions of keeping it. Is there anyone or anything out there that cares for the suffering of the brokenhearted?*

"Honey, could you show me where you keep your coffee?" I could hear his rich familiar voice, giving real question to my sanity, as he called out to me. "You're out."

As though mesmerized, I followed the invisible path of his intoxicatingly masculine scent that pulled me through the house into the kitchen. No man had the right to smell so good at such great distances. I found myself analyzing his fragrance, his essence. What was that smell anyway? It was like a great cologne, unlike anything the most talented designer could create, mixed with the natural scent of a fresh spring rain. Only nature could create a bouquet so clean and crisp. I stifled a deep sigh as I looked at him, standing there ready for the day. He was leaning casually against the counter, watching his new world outside my window, unaware I'd entered the room. I caught myself almost envying how he made looking good seem all so effortless. He was a perfect picture of a real man. Every hair accounted for, in its ideal place, and a face of an angel. It hit me then that I'd never find another like him. The history-proven fact was that there never has been another man like him. This undeniable awareness allowed fear to needle its way into my heart. If I fell in love with this man, that surely meant loneliness in my future.

I wasn't aware he drank coffee, I realized as he turned toward me, morning sunlight catching the sparkle off his famously blue eyes.

*Just look at that beautiful face I'm now sharing my days with.* How did I get into this situation? He needs to go back now, before I can't let him. It seems like a lifetime ago when this whole mess got started, and yet it's only been days since he stepped into my life. But I know it's only a matter of time before he steps back out. I still remember the day that I now call the first day of my renewed life, when my coworker and travel buddy Heather Dawson called with an offer that started it all.

"Hope you're calling because you have something wickedly fun to purpose . . ." I said into the phone without even bothering to say hello. I was eager to hear any schemes for new adventures she might have up her sleeve.

Heather and I were both flight attendants for a major airline and had been friends since we started our professions at the age of nineteen. Our bond grew early out of our mutual love of both travel and the airline benefits that allowed us to frequently do so—anywhere, anytime.

"Samantha, do I have a trip of a lifetime to offer you."

I held my breath, anticipating a string of thrilling details yet to be shared. Traveling with Heather was always a curious mix of expectation and trepidation.

"Whatcha got?" I said as I took a seat in the chocolate-suede recliner next to the phone station.

I stretched my long legs out in front of me and gave in to the comforts a leisurely chat can bring. I was never more aware of how few people I now had in my life with whom to share such an easy conversation. I remembered how my desire to be interwoven with family and friends had brought me back to my hometown of Atlanta, Georgia, in the first place. Things had been so good in the beginning. I smiled in remembrance of how my phone would ring impatiently with invitations to Sunday dinners that my mother was sure I did not want to miss. I couldn't believe it had been two years since cancer had overcome her and swept her away from me.

Heather's voice hummed in my ear as I struggled against a storm of bad memories insidiously working its way into my mind. The questioning tone of her voice abruptly brought me back from the dark place I was lingering.

"Sam, are you listening to me? Boston in the spring . . ." she said.

My focus flickered as I tried get back into our easy banter. I had no idea how many of the details I'd missed, but the East Coast sounded fabulous. In my head, I was already packing as I contemplated my favorite place to be during the changing of the seasons. No matter if it's winter to spring or summer to fall, I'd never been disappointed when visiting the east. I loved how the crisp morning air would grudgingly give way as the sun came out to warm my bones, an unavoidable reminder that summer was fast approaching.

"Boston? Sounds great. Outside of the airport, I've never seen Boston," I said.

Instantly, I began thinking about digging out my mother's camera. She had loved to capture the changes in nature that were so often taken for granted in every day living.

"Yep, me either. I'd like to make a drive to Salem, too..." Heather paused, then cautiously added, "... if you don't mind."

My experience in Boston might have been limited, but I knew enough about the area and my friend to know this would be another stop on her long list of paranormal destinations.

"It's just one night, Sam." Heather continued, trying to sell the idea as I listened silently.

"Well, one night I could probably handle," I sighed.

I squirmed involuntarily in my chair at the thought of exploring the supernatural and made a mental note not to share any photos with my Baptist—preacher daddy. Not unless I had time for a passionate sermon about trusting God to open your eyes to such things on judgment day and not before.

"That's my girl!" She exclaimed. "See you tomorrow."

As she hung up, I feared I'd gotten into more then I could handle.

My mind shifted gears as I lugged my favorite faded black suitcase out from my crowded closet. It looked dreadful, but every single scratch and ding was a visible reminder of past adventures. Packing for any trip, work or pleasure, was always a time-consuming event for me. As I dug through my wardrobe and looked for something striking, I stumbled across my favorite yellow sundress. If only it was warmer on the East Coast now. I loved how I looked in that dress, so feminine and petite with just a hint of sexual promise in its plunging neckline. I imagined a good bra might help rally up a little more cleavage. Heat rushed to my cheeks from my surprising audaciousness.

Reluctantly, I decided the sundress would have to wait. I picked out a few sweaters and light jackets that would be more practical for early spring weather. I held a blue sweater up to my face and examined myself in the mirror. With my chestnut hair, a gift from my beautiful mother, and the soul-piercing blue eyes of my father, I was aware that men found me attractive. At least until they deemed me unapproachable, usually within the same heartbeat. My initial shyness with strangers, though not my true self, didn't help matters. I vowed this trip to not succumb to that bashfulness that always comes over me when I meet someone new. Unwelcome, uncontrollable, and totally unlike my true self, it worked in cruel tandem with the maddeningly stale cycle that was my current social life.

I threw down the blue sweater and reached for a white one instead. As I examined my wardrobe change in the mirror, I studied my flaws and celebrated my advantages. I'd always wished to be a more voluptuous woman, but was given a petite frame instead. I sighed in resignation. I knew I had no choice but to do the best with what I'd been given. Thirty was looming over me, ready to lower the hammer on my single twenties, and I wondered how much longer I'd be alone. The race with my internal clock was beginning to exhaust me. A ringing phone broke my trance, and I raced to catch it.

"Hello," I answered cheerfully, pleased that for once I had beat that answering machine to the punch.

"This is going to be so much fun. We should be there before noon, and we'll head straight for Salem."

I smiled as Heather's excitement overrode her phone etiquette.

"Sam?"

"Who is this?" I sternly teased. I marveled at all of the pent-up energy that, as always, would keep her up the night before a trip.

"What?" Heather said, confused. Never would it occur to her I might not have known it was her calling.

"I'm only kidding." I laughed. "I'm ready and willing, Captain."

"Well, good, because we're on the early morning flight, and you know what that means . . ." she said. Had it been in person, the statement would have come with a wink and a nudge.

To Heather, all business travelers, especially of the male sort, took that early morning flight to the East Coast. Independently single and also in search of her soul mate, the possibilities seemed endless.

"I wonder if we'll get into first class," she pondered out loud.

"Yes, I'm aware of your early morning philosophy." I tried to sound as excited as she was, but I hated flying that early.

"You *are* leaving the 'man-repeller' at home this time?" She asked me accusingly.

"Don't worry. I don't have it on today." I held back a sigh of impatience. My treasured Elvis souvenir absolutely was going with me, just not around my neck.

"Good, because you remember our last trip . . ."

*There it was*, I thought as I rolled my eyes. I wondered how long before she'd mention her displeasure with our last adventure. I'd bought my lucky charm several years ago during a trip to Memphis. The last time Heather and I flew, it became a conversation piece for two men we had met onboard our flight. They did not find it as precious as I did. After some Elvis-bashing by the two gentlemen, my patience, to quote a phrase, "left the building."

"It wasn't my fault those guys were such jerks." I crossed my free arm around my stomach, tense at the memory.

Exasperated with the subject, I tried to convince her I was not at fault. Unfortunately, their lack of manners and complete lack of understanding had quickly led to an unpleasant and abrupt ending to what Heather had hoped to be a promising connection.

"Why do you always have to wear it when you fly?" She demanded.

"Because it comforts me."

I grew tired of explaining to everyday folk the reasons behind the perfectly normal habits of a true Elvis fan. I've been one since I was eight years old, and nothing was going to change now.

"You're so defensive where he's concerned, I swear, Sam." Heather was losing steam on the argument. She knew she couldn't fight me.

"Well, maybe so, but I'm not leaving it behind." I insisted. "But for you, I'll put it in my pocket so there's no worries."

I was not beyond compromising, but I never flew without my good-luck charm, and I wasn't starting now.

"Good, I'll meet you at the airport first thing in the morning. Wait until you see the books I found about Salem." With that, she promptly hung up.

I stood there and laughed at the dial tone humming in my ear. *She'd forgotten to say good-bye again*, I thought as I hung up and returned to the chore of packing. With hand on hip, I stared at my open bag as if waiting for its assistance to tell me what items I'd forgotten.

After a bit more inventorying, I finally accepted this was the best I was going to do. I closed up my bag and left it strategically placed by my front door. I had been known to walk right out the house in an early morning haze with no bag in hand. My clever planning pleased me, and I smiled all the way back to my bedroom. As I slipped off my light robe and pink bunny slippers, I stretched my arms out into the warm air that the ceiling fan kept circulating above my head. *It's already so hot, and it's only spring*, I thought as I plopped down on my bed. I yawned big, grabbed my down comforter, and banished it to the end of the bed frame.

I reached to the top of my bedside reading stack for the novel that I'd been told was a must-read. I adjusted my pillow and settled back into a mountain of feathers. Pleased with my comfortable arrangement, I paused to look at my diary lying untouched on the nightstand. Cynically I glared at it and noticed the dust now collecting over its paisley stamped leather cover. I hadn't touched it since my mother's passing. It looked so out of place amongst its immaculate surroundings.

Sighing, I rolled over onto my back, relaxed and ready for the good read I'd been looking forward to all evening.

However, satisfying the need for an entertaining diversion quickly began to fade after just a few lines. My arms grew tired of holding sweet pages of distraction, and the comfort of sleep began to consume me. I dropped the book onto the empty pillow beside me and drifted off. A dusty diary full of memories would haunt my dreams.

I woke up startled by my alarm at 4:00 the next morning. As it screamed throughout my bedroom, I found myself regretting that I'd agreed to catch that first flight with Heather. I dragged myself up into a wobbly stance, and my body fought against the idea of rising before the sun was up. My stomach flipped as I headed for my slippers and some hot coffee. I coaxed myself down the hallway to the slap-slap of pink bunny feet on the hardwood floor. My cautious steps only faltered when I jumped in surprise as the phone shrieked in the early stillness.

"Yes."

"Hey there, you're up. Good." Heather's energetic voice didn't even give hint to the fact she'd most likely not slept a wink.

"Yep. Jumping for joy. I'm up."

"Yes, and you sound so cheerful, too." Heather said, laughing at my misery.

"This is the best I can do at four in the morning."

"I'm sure that'll improve with coffee. Just called to make sure you were up. See you at the airport." And with that, she was gone again.

I vowed to seriously speak to her about this hanging up business as I dropped the phone back into its cradle.

\* \* \*

I didn't fully wake up until I pulled into the airport parking lot. As if someone clicked on my internal light switch, I was finally aware of my surroundings. I must have driven the whole way on autopilot again, which wasn't a comforting thought. As if I had some kind of honing device implanted in my very bones, I migrated here like a bird in the clouds headed for southern climate. I didn't bother to lecture myself about unsafe road habits, as that never seemed to help. Instead, I raced to meet Heather at the main ticket counter, as she'd requested.

Heather and I quickly advanced to the gate without having to think through the airport's paces—this part was just another day in our lives. I had to remind myself this was a pleasure trip and not one for work. Like all good and prepared passengers, we had ample time before our flight to inspect the little shops that can ruin a budget even before the trip begins. After acquiring some high-priced snacks, we returned to our gate and blended in with the rest of the waiting crowd. I sat in silence and observed the buzzing energy of my fellow travelers. Some lingered around the check-in counter, determined to be the first in line. Others sat and pretended not to care, all the while keeping a watchful eye out for a gate agent's arrival. I snickered to myself as I considered this ritual was much like a strategic military movement. Hundreds of travelers kick off their adventures simultaneously with the boarding instructions that guide all alike to their respective seats. Only once seated does everyone on board have strict orders to begin their vacations.

I shook my head at my own imagination and turned my attention to the books Heather had brought about Salem's infamous history. With its population now standing at more than 40,000 and rising, Salem had risen dramatically from its small-village past of legendary acts of cruelty that are still discussed in history classes today. Goose bumps rose up on my arms as I was reminded of how the quaint beginnings of Salem in 1626 degenerated into the witch-hunts, trials, and burnings at the stake of the accused.

"This town sounds intense and scary," I admitted as I drug my eyes away from the artist's depiction long enough to look up at Heather.

"That was a long time ago. It should be interesting to see what it's become now." Heather's eyes never left the magazine she'd found discarded in the boarding lounge.

I narrowed my eyes to better examine the object of her interest. I peeked at the issue date and chuckled. I'd read that same edition while on the job at least three times last week out of sheer boredom. Just as I was about to make a sarcastic comment about how she might be spending her down time on duty, the gate agent made his imperious arrival. He wasted little time before starting in with the boarding announcements, and we stepped into line with the first class passengers bound for the East Coast. While I assumed Heather was contemplating who might be worthy of a good conversation during flight, I thought more about sleep and yawned.

I looked around casually at this morning's first-class travel mix. Predictably, it consisted mostly of businessmen who importantly carried black briefcases and sat in front to escape the woes of coach class. But there was one lone traveler standing with a big smile and too many carry-on bags who caught my eye. I had her pegged within five seconds as a first-time, first-class traveler. She was about my age and certainly seemed as friendly as she could be. She stood excitedly behind me in line.

"I've never flown in first class before," she said as she tapped me on my shoulder to get my attention.

"Oh? Well, there's a first time for everything," I offered with a weak smile.

"The alcohol is free, right?" She asked me as she adjusted a large, pink floppy hat. I would have been willing to bet she wore quite often.

"Yes, it is. But if they run out, ask her," I said and pointed in Heather's direction. "She probably has a stash of minis with her right now."

"What?" Heather said, sensing she'd become part of the conversation.

"This is my first time," the excited women told Heather.

"Congratulations." Heather said and forced a smile as she turned back around.

I chuckled and imagined Heather's eyes rolling back inside her head over my new friend's exuberance. I liked her, right down to her plastic gardening shoes that matched that pink, droopy hat. She had flare, and I applauded her for being her true self. Whatever that really was, I was not sure.

Our flight was on time and uneventful, just the way a flight should be. As expected, Heather chatted with the man in front of us, and I slept the whole way to Boston, only to be awakened when the landing gear again touched ground. I stretched and thought how a nap on a plane is the best way to get from point A to point B in the blink of an eye. Like I imagined time travel to be, a flight could be over just shortly after it started.

As we deplaned, Heather and I felt at home in middle of the noisy crowd at the gate. After I made quick goodbyes to my new friend, we quickly moved through the terminal. We rolled our trusty carry-on bags and exchanged smiles as we sailed past a tense crowd at baggage claim. Before long, we had stepped up to a rental car counter, and a handsome young man ran us through the ritual. We cut him short when he got to directions, and instead headed straight for our adventure. We were well-traveled, why would we find Boston any different to navigate than most large cities?

Heather guided our rental car out from the garage and into the spring sun, still low in a pale eastern sky. The air was crisp and the sun warm on our windows as we jumped onto the freeway that would lead us to Salem. Heather weaved into the hectic traffic, coaxing our rental car into wide lanes full of locals rushing off to their appointments for the day. I marveled at how quickly drivers had to think to make an exit or miss other drivers trying to do the same. Heather loved to drive fast, but I could see her fingers turning white on the steering wheel as our speed escalated. I gripped the sides of my seat in fear. My stomach began to turn.

"You know, it would be okay if we got there in one piece," I said as she weaved in and out of traffic, which was actually going too slow for her taste.

"I've got it under control. This traffic is slower than the outskirts of Arkansas, 'cause Yankees can't drive," she laughed.

As Heather made a move into the right lane to avoid a slower driver, I squinted disbelievingly through a sun-blurred windshield. I sucked in my breath as I saw that our lane was quickly narrowing to a close with no room to merge. As if I was driving, I glanced over my left shoulder at the solid line of traffic that moved tightly by us. My heart began to race as I again looked forward. The end of the lane was coming fast with what looked like construction barrels blocking us from even using the shoulder. I started to yell my standard alarm.

"Heather, Heather, Heather, Heather!" I screamed, as if her name alone was warning enough.

"I got it, I got it, I got it!"

Everything slowed to one-quarter time as Heather's foot hit the brake. Her right arm came across my chest, like a mother protecting her child. Her well-intentioned gesture was no match for the sheer force of my body as I hurled toward the car's dash. Despite Heather's foot still buried on the brake, our car plowed headlong through the blockade. Orange water-filled barrels splattered their load in our wake. I dimly registered the thud of my forehead hitting the dash before I fell back into my seat.

After who knows how much time had passed, I realized we'd come to a stop. With my head pounding, I sat back and watched the spots float around in front of my blurred eyes. Are we okay? Is the rental okay? I looked over at Heather, who was secure in her seatbelt and staring at the never-ending flow of traffic that couldn't be bothered with such trifle things as an accident.

"You okay?" To speak was debilitating, and I winced at the pain. Already I was sure everything was going to hurt for days to come.

"They didn't even stop," said Heather, not quite focused on our immediate well-being.

Just as I was about to point out the miracle of our survival, I realized she was absolutely right. Not one car had even slowed, much less actually stopped. I found myself looking around in earnest, thinking that surely someone would stop eventually. It was as if nobody even noticed us as they continued down the freeway. Had we crashed right through the space-time continuum? Could people today really be so heartless?

We hadn't been in Boston but an hour, and already we'd had a serious mishap. I was beginning to wonder if this wasn't a bad sign that would follow us throughout the trip.

"They must notice that we're in one piece," I tried to offer up for comfort.

"Your head!" Heather's eyes widened as she pointed toward my already pounding cranium.

"Am I bleeding?" I reached up and with one touch felt a rush of pain between my eyes.

"No, but you're going to have a huge bump." She leaned forward to inspect my unsightly development. "I'm guessing that could teach anyone about seat belts."

"Why, thank you for all of your concern, friend," I said and tried to match her sarcastic tone. "Shall we get off the side of the road?"

Considering our rocky start on the Massachusetts freeway system, I counted us lucky that the car not only started, but also went on to transport us to our destination.

Soon Heather eased our now rattling car into the small town of Salem. My head was pounding less, but my hands continued to shake involuntarily. Heather's knuckles regained color as she loosened her grip on the steering wheel. Even she was glad to see the diminished traffic that downtown Salem brought. The slower pace eased my flustered nerves as well, though I was sure I would at least need some aspirin before the day was over.

The courtyards in the center of town had a historic feel of another period. Even the businesses had facades that harkened back to the town's historical beginnings. I admired the detail work in the construction of the faded red-brick buildings and narrow roads. A horse-drawn carriage in this town would not have surprised me at all.

All too soon, we were reminded of Salem's dark history as we passed the Witch Dungeon Museum at the center of town. Posters on the front of the building advertised the displays inside of the torture devices and dungeons of that period. I shuddered at the lack of reverence for those who suffered—just come on in and see the artifacts. The invitation was as open as one would offer to give a tour of their home. The building looked dark and evil to me with its shadowy doorways and iron guarded windows.

As we continued on, I noticed the local youth, lounging on benches in the local graveyards as if they were in a park. They chatted casually while sipping designer coffees, sitting amongst the dead in customary tranquility.

"Did you see that? They're hanging out in the graveyards like it's the mall."

Heather looked the direction I was pointing, but didn't reply.

"That'll be the day." I said.

As was my travel assignment, I continued to read directions as Heather took the final turn down a narrow gravel driveway. Our battle-worn car creaked to a grateful stop in front of a beautiful Victorian-era bed and breakfast. Relieved to get out of the vehicle that almost took our lives, I stretched as Heather opened the trunk.

The Crescent Inn was a stately two-story home that had been restored to its original 1906 condition. I marveled at the smallest details in hand-carved wood trim around the windows. We walked up front stairs that creaked with age, but I noticed had been newly painted. The front door was unusually tall and opened into a cozy lobby with maroon velvet high-back chairs and couches of the period stationed around a large stone fireplace. I marveled at a lion's head that was chiseled out of stone, much like something seen in an old horror movie. It was gothic meets Victorian, right before my eyes.

The deep-brown wooden floors groaned as we approached a grand mahogany check-in counter. Behind it was our tiny, bent hostess, her frail body in contrast with the huge piece of lumber she hid behind. A stubby pencil was tucked into her short silver hair. She acknowledged us with a welcoming smile.

"Hello, ladies, how can I help you?" She asked courteously.

"We have a reservation for Dawson," Heather said.

"One moment, please." She turned away to thumb through a file where reservations were kept the old-fashioned way, on hand-written slips stored alphabetically.

"Take your time, Rose," Heather said, using the name on our hostess' time-worn nametag pinned to her shirt. Rose only smiled at Heather's forward nature.

As we waited, I wandered to the other side of the room. Heather finished the business of checking us in as I stopped and lingered over photos of a family posing in front of this grand house. The pictures hung two-by-two on walls that were covered in cream-colored flowered wallpapered. I had to lean in to see through the dingy color of time threatening to overcome the photos that displayed discouraged faces. The captured posed unnaturally. I imagined from their determination to tolerate the photo technology of that period. My eye followed around the frames' dark edges of hand-crafted wood and fell still upon an engraving that read "Haunted Home, 1906."

I shook my head as I started to piece together why Heather had chosen these accommodations: this catered perfectly to her love of ghosts. I snickered thinking what she might actually do if she really had a true paranormal experience. I, on the other hand, would be just fine if I never had one. My train of thought was broken when I heard Rose address Heather, apparently finishing up with her duties.

"Ms Dawson, our famous room eight is ready for you a bit earlier then normal, if you ladies would like to get settled in now?"

I returned to Heather's side. She had to have felt my eyes burning a hole through her. She pretended to not feel it as she signed the final paperwork without making any eye contact.

"Thank you, Rose." Heather said and grabbed her bag, smirking slightly at my irritation she headed for the stairs leading us to our "famous room."

"What exactly is so famous about room eight, Heather?"

"Now, Sam, it's not as bad as you're imagining," she tried reasoning with me. "The room just has a history of being a tad haunted, and I thought since we were in town, we'd get its full effect."

The last time I'd gone along with one of Heather's ghost outings, we ended up in some old hotel in the middle of Arkansas.

"You seem to forget Arkansas."

"Sam, the medium in that hotel told you the ghosts were not hostile," she reminded me defensively.

"You don't find it odd at all that we stayed in a hotel that had a medium as regular staff?" I said and crossed my arms defiantly.

"There was no harm done, Sam." Heather said. "It was all in good fun."

Heather and I did not share the same upbringing that had formed our adult beliefs. Heather was from a wealthy Alabama family that welcomed new ideas and other beliefs. Consequently, Heather was open to experiencing all things with no fear. Conversely, my middle-class, preacher's kid upbringing led by the much more strict Pastor and Mrs. Bennett of Georgia was less flexible. However, our respect for each other's differences was what made our friendship work. That's not to say it was easy, but it was worth it.

"You know I prefer to leave these things where they belong." I told her. I fully believed what my daddy used to say about the other side. It's on the other side for a reason, and it's God's business to handle, not mine.

"Sam," Heather tried to reason with me. "We've done this before."

"Yes, but it's different now. I'd never known anyone who had . . . passed." My voice lowered in embarrassing emotion, and I almost couldn't finish.

Heather's eyes softened as she considered what I'd just said. Without a word, she headed back to the huge mahogany desk to explain to Rose why we couldn't stay. In compassion, Rose called around until she found us another room in a newer, un-haunted hotel nearby.

After another regrettable loading of our rental car, we pulled into a more modern hotel and quickly got checked in. The front desk manager, a man in his forties working in an environment less inspiring then the last, advised us we had an hour before our room would be ready. Meanwhile, Heather had spotted some shops across the street from our new hotel, so we headed out on foot to soak in some local color and flare.

The sun was high in the new spring sky. The apple trees were in bloom and displayed vibrant colors of pink amongst dark green foliage. Whether on the West or the East side of our country, one cannot beat the show Mother Nature puts on with every tree in bloom. I paused to take in the golden sun shining warmly on my face, enticing me to kick off my shoes and walk barefoot in a nearby park. Reluctantly, I abandoned the notion and instead chose to follow the ever-focused Heather into the first tourist shop she spotted.

The endless display of trinkets in one of these stores was enough to make anyone shop on autopilot. I stopped at the first display rack of key chains, as there was too many to really look at them all, and wondered if anyone actually collected them for travel memories. It was only in Memphis, surrounded with everything Elvis, that a store like this made any sense to me. I chuckled at my clearly biased opinion. Key chains and refrigerator magnets seem to be this store's specialty.

I was just about to suggest we go somewhere else when I noticed Heather staring out the window in the back of the store. I assumed she was bored and called out to her that we should move on. As I approached her, I noticed what had caught her eye.

*Mystic Books.* The bright red sign drew Heather like a proverbial moth to a flame. Although the store was clearly open, the sign was the only beacon to signal visitors to its tucked-away location on a side cobblestone street. It seemed hidden away like a gem that only the locals new about. Its location struck me as peculiar as I realized it was only visible from the nick-knack store where we stood. The buildings around it appeared to be empty but available for lease—no doubt because of location, they would stay that way for some time.

"Strange, it seems hidden almost," I mentioned, puzzled

We left the first shop to walk around to the bookstore. As we approached, I could see another smaller advertisement: *Fortunes told and sold inside*. Sold? I had never seen such an offer, and I will admit I was intrigued. Without hesitating, Heather ventured in and left me standing outside the frosted privacy doors. I quickly followed and was greeted by the sound of an entrance bell and the overwhelming sight of books stacked from the floor to the ceiling. The aroma of burning candles smelled like lavender and weakly masked the odor of molding paper. *My mother loved that scent*, I thought as I lingered in the entrance, unsure of my purpose or direction. I stretched my neck to look around, but could not spot my friend anywhere. She was already lost amongst the many books.

While I decided which way to go, I noticed a blue line on the hardwood floor. My eyes clung in hesitation to the painted floor marker that yearned for me to follow it. The idea that direction was needed to keep from getting lost inside the maze was intimidating enough to keep me cemented in my spot.

"Heather?" I whispered, unwilling to move.

I had no idea whom I might disturb but in a place like this, anyone could be in here. I waited and played with the buttons of my light spring jacket. No response came back from within the rows of books.

Small, crudely handwritten signs marked each isle's specialty. A shiver ran down my back at the one before me that read *spells and potions*. For the second time that day, I was again uncomfortable. Even if God and I were not on speaking terms, I had always believed He was watching, even when I was a child. God had especially been ratting me out to my father my whole life. I never knew what I feared more, God's wrath or my father's, and I was raised to dread the wrath of both. As a child, I always ran to my mother to hide from their assumed opposing judgment against me. I often wondered if that is why God took her from me. Was he trying to flush me out from all of my hiding places?

Just as I proceeded to move, I heard a book hit the floor, and profanity soon followed.

"Shit, shit, shit!"

"Heather?" I again whispered.

"What are you whispering for? Damn it, my foot!"

I followed a steady stream of vulgarity and found my friend a row away. Seated on the dirty floor, she was inspecting her foot. I noticed her open toed sandals had been thrown aside in haste. The massive dusty novel that was responsible for her discomfort sat binder side up, too dirty for me to make out it's title.

"Dropped a book on your foot, did you?" I have always found humor in the obvious.

"No I did not! I wasn't touching that book, it just fell off the shelf." Heather didn't look up from her throbbing limb.

"Hmm, well maybe our hotel ghost followed us here?" I offered.

"I'm in real pain here, Sam, do you mind?"

Though Heather was always the brave one, she could not handle the smallest amount of physical discomfort. Pain and dirt were Heather's enemies. I held back a giggle and inspected the dirt that now clung to Heather's once white posterior. This was not the time to point out the condition of her favored capri pants.

"Sorry, you just look so funny down there."

Heather briskly stood up, swiping at long blonde hairs that clung to her face. She brushed herself off and took a moment to inventory her condition. Obviously not finding the event as funny as I had and satisfied nothing was broken, she returned to the business at hand.

"Did you see the sign coming in?" Heather quickly changed the subject.

"You mean 'fortunes told and sold'," I replied cautiously. I could already guess where this was going.

"Isn't that mysterious? I've never seen anything like it."

"Sounds like a hook for tourist fish to me." I did not feel like being lunch for the local fishers.

"Well, we're here, and we are tourists. 'When in Rome, do as the Romans do'." she said.

In Rome, Italians spend the mid-day break in the town square, not in small musty bookstores getting ready to purchase a fortune. I was annoyed, but to explain that difference would be pointless. Heather's pleading green eyes told me she'd already made one sacrifice for me today, and now I needed to return the gesture.

Heather headed out with me in tow to find a clerk for the so-called fortune readings. The purchase counter was partially hidden in the dimly lit back of the store. Dust particles floated lazily in the slim strips of light that filtered in through the lowered mini-blinds. Like a trusty hound dog, that once nerve-racking blue line led us to the counter. As Heather rang the service bell, I made note that the same blue line continued past the desk and presumably led to an exit. Maybe it was the flight attendant in me, or the scared rabbit, but knowing my exit brought me great comfort.

We only had to wait a few minutes before we were introduced to Lady Sharone, as she asked us to call her. She entered the room with her head held high, shoulders back, but giving off no airs of callousness. I couldn't help but stare at her. Briefly, she paused to look over some papers. We took that moment to overcome our preconceived ideas of what a woman in her position should look like. By the look on Heather's astonished face, I could tell we both had imagined gypsies from our fairytales. Instead, she was professionally dressed, straight from Saks Fifth Avenue in a loose-fitting tan skirt, black boots, and a snappy white blouse. She only stood at about 5'0" and was stocky with an authoritative persona. Something about her presence immediately put me on my best behavior, in spite of my skepticism. When she spoke, the voice of an angel flowed to our ears. Her words drifted on soft low tones that added to her sophistication.

"Hello ladies. What is your wish today?" She asked with a smile. We stared back, both of us stunned into silence that did not seem to bother her.

"Hello. We were visiting your town today and noticed your sign out front." Heather spoke first. I nodded in agreement.

Lady Sharone didn't ask which sign, rather she seemed to know. She asked us to follow her into a more private room where we could talk. My once sacrificial act of friendship to follow against my own convictions had taken me to a crossroads. My need to discover why I felt so drawn to her prevailed, and I went willingly.

We entered the back room and arranged ourselves around a small ornate coffee table with characters etched along its side that I could not read. The room was casually decorated with warm green and brown tones. I wondered about her background and why she didn't decorate in the more traditional Victorian colors, keeping in sync with the town's hues of blue and maroon. Soft lighting glowed in the corners of the room, and no round tables with the crystal ball from my fantasy were to be found. Lady Sharone motioned for us to take a seat on a high back couch made out of cedar that had over-stuffed cushions for comfort. She was the first to speak as we attempted to settle in for the duration, our bodies sunk into plush mounds. After the day we'd had up to this point, I could have slept there.

"You wish to speak with me?" She said and looked directly at Heather, who got right to the point.

"I'm looking for my purpose, my future I suppose, and I was curious about your offer out front."

"I see," she paused before adding, "To find your purpose is a lifelong journey. However, the opportunity to discover it can always be close."

"I understand foretelling someone's future, but I don't grasp the 'fortunes told and sold' sign out front," said Heather.

Lady Sharone only smiled at her.

"Uh, mostly the 'sold' part," Heather nervously pointed out.

"My dear, one can't buy their fortune like shopping for new clothes, only satisfied until the perfect outfit is found."

She paused to see if we were following her before she continued.

"One may find this foretold future does not follow the fairytale they were dreaming of. Unfortunately I still have to collect my fees even though I 'sold' them a story they did not want to hear," she clarified.

I started to feel the swindle build and could not help but fidget. The couch suddenly was not nearly as comfortable as when I'd first sat down. The madam's gaze left Heather and was now resting on me.

"What is your name, dear?" She asked suddenly.

"Samantha."

Lady Sharone fell silent as If there was more for me to say. I struggled for words as the madam waited for more.

"Uh, my friends call me Sam."

"Samantha. That's a name with an old soul behind it." The madam continued to keep her eyes locked on me as she addressed Heather. "What is yours, dear?"

I slowly nudged Heather, who was unaware she was being spoken to.

"Heather. My friends call me Heather."

I smiled coyly, realizing Heather had spoken my exact words. It's not often my friend was lacking for words of her own. Slowly, the madams' eyes left mine and went to Heather's.

"I see."

Lady Sharone explained that for twenty dollars each, she could help us discover our future. I was well familiar with that look of hopeful curiosity in my friend's eyes. There was no way Heather would walk away now with the key to the unknown dangling right before her. All she had to do was invest twenty dollars and she'd find out how good or how bad her future was destined to be.

I did not believe a word of it. Heather put her money up on the table. I reached into my pocket for twenty dollars and consented to play along. I laid the money next to Heather's, determined to return the same consideration she'd given to me earlier in the day. Heather smiled at what she knew was an effort for me to accept the unacceptable. Lady Sharone interrupted our bonding moment of one for all, all for one.

"There is one warning I will need to share with you." When she felt she had our attention, she continued. "If you're not ready, I cannot help you see your way down any path."

Disappointed, I reached up and took my money off the table. The madam's eyes fell upon me in disapproval, but my main concern was for Heather's feelings. I smiled and extended my arm to indicate the two of them should proceed. Heather's money remained on the table, and I settled back into the couch to watch the show.

Lady Sharone asked Heather if she had anything that was close and personal. She dug around in her purse and pulled out a small flower-etched locket I had never seen before. As Lady Sharone then instructed, Heather obediently closed her eyes, held the locket between the palms of her hands, and began to meditate.

I watched as Lady Sharone glided across the room, well versed in her act. She required only a few moments to dim the lights and spark a few candles. The soft light cascaded our shadows onto the walls behind us, and a smell of vanilla was soon in the air. The mood was now relaxed and tranquil, and I felt my eyes getting heavy from the stress of our day as every cell screamed for some much-needed rest. Enjoying my descent even further into the couch, not willing to terminate this serene feeling, I slipped my hands into my front pockets. My fingertips gently traced my favored souvenir resting there at the bottom. I traced down to its point, where it stung my finger, but I did not recoil. I concentrated on the feel of solid gold as my eyes got heavier. The madam started to lightly sing a song in a language I did not recognize. The last thing I consciously observed through the small slits that were now my eyes was the madam's concentrated gaze. Once again, those eyes settled on me. Her look was intense, but my fatigue was overcoming. The smell of vanilla candles was all around me as I drifted into a dreamland.

I floated for a while in that magical place so many describe when first dozing: that heavy feeling somewhere between consciousness and sleep. I could hear a beeping noise keeping perfect rhythm somewhere within the fog that consumed me. It seemed to beep in sync with the beat of my heart, and it was surprisingly comforting. Along with the rhythmic beat, I could hear muffled conversation in voices I did not recognize. I tried to open my eyes, but found them unwilling, as if someone or something held them shut. I'd never experienced a dream quite like this one. Oddly, I was not scared.

I was startled awake by the sound of a front desk bell that signaled another curiosity seeker had arrived. Sitting upright, I suppressed a yawn and tried not to make it too obvious that I had fallen asleep. Lady Sharone excused herself to tend to the new customer at hand.

"Well, did you find what you were looking for?" I asked Heather, as if I'd been listening all along. Heather watched as I awkwardly held back the need to stretch.

"You couldn't hear for yourself?" Her tone suggested it was not a secret I had been asleep.

"I'm sorry, but she lost me at the 'If your soul is not meant to go that path' crap."

Our conversation was interrupted by our hostess' return. A blush washed over my face as the word 'crap' still seemed to linger in the room. She once again took her seat at the table with Heather.

"I apologize for the delay. Shall we continue?" She asked.

Lady Sharone breathed deeply and lowered her gaze to the tabletop. Time seemed to slow as Heather and I now sat in the uncomfortable silence caused by the dissenting comments we both seemed to wonder if she'd heard. Heather was still clutching the locket when the madam finally looked up.

"Sometimes love is lost for reasons we don't understand." Her unreadable gaze rested on me briefly before turned back to Heather. "Such experiences can either help us grow closer to finding our true purpose or stifle our walk down that path all together. It is in these times when support can be sent from unexpected sources."

Again the madam returned her eyes to me. I fiddled with the hem on the sides of the cushions and pretended not to notice.

"Believe me when I say someone special is coming to help you find your way back onto your righted path."

Heather's eyes lit up. I had seen that look before. Usually it coincided with the appearance of a new man in her life. So, that was it? I couldn't believe men were the most enlightened prediction our hostess could offer. She did not say it would be a man per se, but I considered it was probably easy for Lady Sharone to see we were both still searching for love. Heather took as much joy in the relationship as she did the hunt. I smirked at that fact. Surely this had been what our hostess had easily seen. She told Heather exactly what she wanted to hear. After all, if the relationship did not work out, it would be easy to say he was not meant to be with her on this path of life. I could tell by the wide-eyed look of hope on Heather's face she was hooked with the idea.

"Lady Sharone, exactly when can she expect this person to arrive?" I could not help but push the envelope just a little.

"You'll have to excuse my friend, she's always been a skeptic where people of your profession were concerned."

"If you'll pardon me, I think I will excuse myself. Thank you for your time."

I rose quickly to leave before Heather could protest. Grabbing my oversized handbag, I slipped it over one shoulder and headed for the door. My prediction was that I would say something regrettable if I stayed. Most importantly, I could no longer handle the way our hostess had been inspecting me, as if trying to peer inside my very soul. Truth be known, I had been more afraid of what she might find there if she looked too hard. Though I did not believe this meeting was anything more then a show at the time, there was a sense of aptitude in her eyes when she looked at me. I ignored the possibility that Lady Sharone might have been given some insight. As I exited the room, I nearly upset a massive stack of books. I caught my balance before spilling into a waiting customer.

"Oh," I sputtered as my breath caught in my throat. *Get a grip*, I thought sternly. "Hello. I'm sure my friend will be out soon, and we won't hold you up long."

"Oh, no problem. I'm in no hurry, and she's worth waiting for," answered the woman cheerfully.

"Really? Are you a regular here?" I had to ask.

"Oh, yes. I see her a few times a month. She has been helping me to expand my vision."

Internally I rolled my eyes, but I was brought up to be polite, so I refrained from giving her my thoughts on the matter.

"I see. That must be a great relief to you." I tried to muster up a sincere response, but the stranger's eyes narrowed, and I did not know what to say. "I mean, to see and all, after not being able to see."

I had no idea where I was going, but I was sinking for sure.

"Yes, well it was nice speaking with you." I headed off into the rows of books, regretting I'd responded at all. I looked for a place to hide and wait out my friend's session.

Quite some time later, Heather finally exited Lady Sharone's sanctuary. She found me sitting patiently, a *People* magazine in hand. She bounced on air, uplifted and light on her feet. Her face radiated happiness.

"So, you're good to go then?" I offered, silently hoping we could now leave this place.

"I know you're ready to leave, Sam. I thank you for going along with that for my benefit."

I paused before replying and tried to assess any hint of sarcasm, but found none. I realized how truly happy my friend looked.

"Did she tell you all about the great man you'll meet, and how he'll sweep you off your feet in grand style?" I asked.

Though I was trying to push buttons good naturedly, Heather would not take the bait. She said Lady Sharone was a caring person who truly seemed to know what was in everyone's heart of hearts. Heather told me that though I had not paid, she had spoken to her about me. Lady Sharone had said she felt some deep anger was stifling me. I needed to be moved by the power of love before I could overcome the chains that now bind me.

Her words rang true in my heart. As we left the bookstore, I sensed that something had changed. I couldn't place a finger on it, but the sky seemed a brighter blue as we walked side-by-side back to our hotel. Maybe I did need someone to come along and wake up my heart from its deep slumber. I pushed back tears, wondering how Lady Sharone could have seen what I could not even admit to myself. I decided to rest in the knowledge that she felt someone was coming. Deep down I'd hoped she was right.

# CHAPTER 2

A return to Atlanta meant going back to the reality of every day life. In the simple act of living, I'm reminded of my mother's absence. Our daily habit had been to call each other at least once, but usually twice, a day. No matter how late I'd arrive in a city, once at my hotel, I'd call her so we could talk one last time before retiring for the night. She'd never again call just to check in with her baby girl and see that all was okay in my world. Though nothing could change that, I realized while in Salem that it was time to make an effort to discover my way without her. Just how to do that, I wasn't sure. But before long, I had found myself lulled into an accepting rhythm of life that consisted mostly of work. Soon that special someone Lady Sharone had spoken about was long forgotten.

After a three-day trip of screaming babies and bad turbulence, I was headed down an Atlanta freeway, unaware of the changes yet to come to my life. I drove with the convertible top down, lost in thoughts of a hot shower and apple cinnamon candles. My cares seemed to blow away in the warm southern breeze that tousled my dark hair. With each mile I could feel the days' stress melt away as the humming of a German-made engine carried me closer to my home.

As I turned onto my street, I passed professionally manicured yards on every corner. My car eased through the winding streets, leading me home like a horse that knows the way back to the barn for feeding time. That hot shower was now just minutes away.

Gearing the engine down to a low wind, I waved at Mrs Jefferson as I pulled into the driveway. My friendly neighbor waved back, arms full of mail she'd just claimed from her box. I smiled remembering the day she excitedly brought the dreadful artifact home from a Saturday flea market spree some years back. Looking at my watch, I chuckled that it read 3:30 p.m. You could set your watch to Mrs. Jefferson's mail check, and I often did just that. Today my watch was right on the money.

"Hello there Mrs Jefferson," I called to her as I got out of my car. I pulled out that same worn luggage and headed to my front door.

"Hello, there, Ms. Sam!" Mrs. Jefferson shouted out.

"How's Mr. Jefferson today?"

Both in their eighties, every day was a new story of health conditions they loved to chat about. I never grew tired of hearing about her bad hip and Mr. Jefferson's bad leg. I figured it made her feel good to tell someone, as their kids never visited.

"His leg is acting up a bit, you know." She shook her head. "He's been sittin' on that couch plum near all day."

"Yes, ma'am. Must be a good ball game on TV," I said. We both laughed at the common knowledge that Mr. Jefferson's ailments got worse on game days.

"I know that's the truth."

"Take care, now Mrs. Jefferson!" I yelled as I opened the door to my cozy, three-bedroom brick beauty that made me feel welcome every time I stepped through its squeaky front door.

"You, too, Ms. Sam."

I barely heard her as I was already inside. The air conditioning was running to cool an unusually hot spring day. I closed the front door but left it unlocked. It was wonderful to feel so safe in my neighborhood. My bag never made it far as I abandoned it in the living room and kicked off my shoes.

Whistling, I headed straight for that shower that had been on my mind the whole drive home. As if in a single motion, I turned on the water and lit the candles I had on display on a bathroom shelf. *I love the scent of apple cinnamon*, I thought as I disrobed and flipped off the lights. Soon I found myself under the warm cascading water I had been longing for. Steam filled up quickly within my sanctuary. I lingered there, enjoying its embrace. Music from a song I'd heard during the drive home echoed in my mind. I hummed along as I ran through the shower rituals that only females understand.

Doused with peach-scented body wash, I lost track of the time. I stretched one long leg out in front of me and bathed from my red painted toenails up to my matching fingertips with a soft washcloth. Feeling of a fresh new spirit, I reached over and shut off the water. Brushing back my long hair, I postponed the inevitable and stood lingering within the warmth that still encircled me. Finally I gave in and cracked the shower door ever so slightly. I cringed from the expected sting of the unwelcome cold air and hurriedly searched for a warm towel.

Wrapped up tight, I was dripping onto the bathroom rug when I heard footsteps pass just outside my refuge. I tried to control my breathing that naturally escalated, but told myself I had to be mistaken. Quietly, I opened the bathroom door to another dramatic temperature change that captured both my breath and my attention. My heartbeat echoed inside my ears, and cold chills ran up my arms. I looked both ways up and down the hallway. Nobody could walk down that hardwood hall without making noise. One even could hear the soft thud of bare feet on that wood.

Just as I was about to give up on my crazy notion of a trespasser, I heard a clear noise coming from the kitchen. Turning quickly towards the sound, I saw the shadow of a figure as it crossed the kitchen entrance. I stared in disbelief. This time, I had not imagined it. There was someone in my house. Fear welled up in me and froze me in the spot I stood.

From my vantage point, I quickly scanned the living room for the phone. Three handsets in the house, and not one of them was within easy, stealthy reach. I had to get to the phone and call 911, but I was uncertain my unwanted guest would stay in the kitchen. I took a steadying deep breath and stepped out ever so quietly into the hallway. With a little hesitation, I crossed the floor and headed for the office and the phone I knew lay inside. Closing the door, I glanced back in time to see the intruder's shadow once again move from one side of the kitchen to the other. I covered my mouth before the scream could come out and locked the office door ever so gently. No longer shivering from cold but from my distress, I raced for the phone.

"911, what is your emergency?" A female voice said.

"I have an intruder in my house, please help me!" I half-croaked into the phone, struggling to keep my voice to a whisper.

"Ma'am, are you residing at 1300 El Camino Street?" The lady asked in a smooth and even tone.

"Yes, yes!"

"A unit is on the way, ma'am, and I will stay on the line with you until it arrives. Are you the only one in the house, ma'am?" She asked flatly.

"Yes, I am alone, I live alone," I explained in a whisper. I never took my eyes off the doorknob. As if in a horror movie, I expected it to move at any minute.

"You saw this person, ma'am?" She asked.

"I saw a shadowy figure of someone in my kitchen and then heard them." I grabbed a letter opener laying on my desk.

"Where are you now, ma'am?"

"I'm calling you from my office."

"The officers should be arriving at your house within minutes, ma'am."

I squatted down next to my desk, still clutching my weapon of choice and unsure of how much damage a letter opener could really do upon an intruder. I looked around in a panic for anything more menacing. In frustration I realized the only weapon in this room was in an Elvis photo that hung on my wall. He posed there smiling back at me in a black velvet suite all the while presenting a large, dangerous looking rifle. *Sure, he has a weapon of action as I squat here with nothing but a letter opener.* Where was Elvis when a girl needed him? I shook my head in disgust over my helpless circumstances.

The few minutes that felt like hours passed until finally I heard a car pull up outside my window. Crawling on my knees, still clutching a phone and my weapon, I scooted over to my window to peek out my blinds. Unwilling and unable to let go of the letter opener, I used its sharp tip to part the blinds. I was finally able to exhale the breath I'd been holding since my escape from the bathroom. Two young men from the Atlanta police department stepped up to my front door. One officer was large and bulky, as if he spent all of his off time pumping iron. I was relieved at the thought of my intruder meeting Mister Iron, as I decided to call him. The still-calm voice of the 911 operator brought me back to the situation at hand.

"Ma'am, officers have arrived at your house."

"Yes, I can see . . ."

"They say your front door is unlocked. Do you give them permission to enter your house, ma'am?" She interrupted.

"Yes, of course!"

"Alright. Please remain in the room, ma'am. They will come to you."

I heard the police announce their arrival as they entered, but no sound of any struggle followed. My legs wavered, weak from a lack of circulation as I tried to stand.

Quietly, I waited next to the desk, still unwilling to release my weapon.

"Ma'am, the officers are saying your home is clear, and you can come out of your room." Her shrill voice rang in my ears. "Nobody was found inside your house, ma'am."

The operator's words kept running through my mind as I sat in disbelief.

"Ma'am, are you still with me?"

"Sorry. Yes, I am. Nobody was in my home," I repeated. "Thank you for helping me. I'll go outside and speak with the officers now."

"Alright, mama, glad I could help."

"Yes, thank you." I hung up and heard knocks at my office door.

"Ma'am, this is the Atlanta police department. It is okay for you to exit the room," called a deep voice.

I opened the door to Mister Iron and a less significant officer, who smiled in calm confidence at me. I look down the hallway toward the kitchen and hesitated to come out.

"It's okay, ma'am. Nobody is in your house." The diminutive partner spoke up. Visions of Barney Fife bounced into my head. I wondered if he felt safe riding around all day with Mister Iron by his side.

"We've checked inside thoroughly, and officers are now checking the grounds," said Officer Thompson, a.k.a. Mister Iron, with a warm smile.

I cautiously opened the door and stepped out into the hallway. As the towel around me loosened, I clutched the wrap tightly to me. Officer Thompson averted his eyes politely. I ignored his shyness and kept a close watch on the kitchen doorway.

"We, uh, checked all your rooms, ma'am," Officer Thompson stuttered over his own words.

I passed by my guests and headed for the hall closet. Searching for something more substantial to cover in, I barely noticed the more relaxed officers who mingled in my living room. I reached for the closet doorknob and stopped short of opening the door.

"There's nobody in there, ma'am," said one of the officers reassuringly.

Taking a moment to consider my fate if he was wrong, I opened the door. In stealth like movements, I reached out for the rain jacket I'd worn in my New York City stop earlier that day. Quickly wrapping myself up within the garment, I tightened the waist belt seeking comfort. Disappointment soon followed as I realized this less exposed fashion did not ease me as I had hoped it would.

I watched as officer Thompson headed for the kitchen. His job now completed, he laid his clipboard onto the table. He busied himself righting papers and pens I assumed were for my use. I paused at the entrance to my own kitchen, still half expecting to come face to face with my intruder. In quiet but unsure acceptance, I took my seat.

"I know what I saw," I muttered more to myself.

"I'm sorry, ma'am, but we're going to need you to fill out some papers before we can leave."

I sighed in frustration and scanned over the papers the officer scooted in front of me. *I guess they have other people with more pressing problems to attend to*, I thought. A few moments of cordial goodbyes and too soon I was left alone. I didn't bother to get up to see them to the door. The house felt unnervingly quite as I sat at the kitchen table in silence. I looked again for signs of anything misplaced and took some comfort in the appearance of order.

Deciding I could not sit there all day, I exited the kitchen and headed for my bedroom. I tried to move forward with my day more out of need than any real acceptance. As I slowly approached the bathroom, unwilling to just pass it by, I tried to remember if the officers had checked it. I looked inside uneasily. My uniform was undisturbed where I had thrown it aside earlier in haste. I considered the possibility that I had just been overly exhausted.

Taking a deep breath, I entered and stood in the middle of the bathroom. The floor was still wet from my dripping body and was cold on the bottoms of my feet. The candles now burned low. I could smell my favored scent and noticed the afternoon sun peeking through my blinds. The soft lighting made me more nervous then relaxed. Reaching over for the light switch, I caught my likeness in the vintage mirror and laughed in horror. My hair was matted and half-dry, which did nothing to distract from the rain gear I was now wearing. I'd definitely put on a show for Atlanta's finest. My chuckle died in my throat as I squinted and leaned toward the mirror. I took notice of something new in the reflection. A mysterious item hung from the showerhead and I had not left it there. Staring at its unbelievable presence, again my heart picked up pace. I dared not turn around. As long as I was looking at it through a mirror, it did not seem real.

I slowly stepped back towards the shower door, still open from earlier. A gold crucifix pendent, encrusted with diamonds, hung dry and sparkling in what little light was caressing it from my bathroom window. It was the most ornamental item I had ever laid eyes on. Clusters of diamonds lay within its obnoxiously large solid gold frame. The four, possibly five, inch pendent hung on a thick chain that was meant for a man.

Now-familiar fear rose like a cold wave in my chest. My mind raced as I tried to find some logical explanation. The police had said no one had been in my house. My only assurance seemed to be that I had not imagined all this after all. The confirmed knowledge that, in fact, an intruder had invaded my home did nothing to slow my hammering heart. What kind of criminal could afford to leave such an expensive, ornate calling card?

I reached out and touched the item, as if to know for sure it was real. I turned it around to look for any markings that might explain its existence. It was real, this I was sure. If there was one thing a woman knew when she saw them, it was real diamonds. The largest piece of diamond jewelry that I had ever touched now rested comfortably in my cupped little hands. I rolled it around and watched the light bounce off this amazing piece of art. Beads of reflection shimmered in color on my bathroom wall. My fear subsided as the mystery of diamonds lay before me.

"Only Elvis could get away with wearing something so . . ."

Words flowed from my mind but were lost in translation and never made the journey to my mouth. *Only Elvis could wear this.* Had I seen this piece of jewelry before? My mind tried to reach out and grab at pieces of a memory that floated just out of reach.

Racing out of the bathroom, jewelry in hand, I headed for my bedroom. I dropped to my knees and jammed my hands under my bed frame. Impatiently, I dug through the piles of books that long ago had overflowed from other shelves in the house. This, of course, included my collection of Elvis-related material. Digging and digging, I knew what I was looking for. Out I pulled the 200-page photo book by a prominent rock photographer. I took no haste in turning the glossy pages as my anxiety levels were rising. Suddenly, I stopped and slowly exhaled. There it was, the picture I had in mind: a particular photograph of Elvis on stage. He stood with an expression of satisfaction upon his face. Head down in a final bow, the trademark white jumpsuit decorated in red flames engulfed his arms as they reached out from his sides. The ensemble was left customarily and provocatively opened at the chest, and there rested an ornate pendant in the shape of a cross.

Though details of the pendent were small, they were identical to that in my hand. I laid the treasure onto the photo page to look for anything that would disprove the obvious. I squinted and tried to bring the small details into view, searching for an explanation. One could plainly see the unmistakable style of what was a one-of-a-kind piece of jewelry.

Time passed in slow motion as I walked, pendent in hand, back to the bathroom. Trying to hold myself together a bit longer, I calmly put the pendent back on the showerhead where I'd found it. I closed the shower door. Maybe I could pretend that it didn't exist. I left the bathroom in a daze and shut the door behind me. Tears streamed down my checks as I held back a chorus of screams that threatened to escape from within me. As if on autopilot, I headed for the kitchen and the biggest knife I could find. Its cold, sharp steal gave me comfort as it rested in my grip. I walked for the kitchen phone and started to dial with shaking hands. With my finger poised to punch the last "1," I stopped.

To call the police again would not get me anywhere. They knew me now as the single women who lived alone with her large imagination. I still had the same problem I had before, no sign of entry. My legs throbbed from my stiff stance. Shaking my legs out, my only thought was of making a phone call to someone who would help me figure this all out. On the third ring, Heather answered the phone.

"Hello."

"Heather." I tried to remain strong, but once I heard her familiar voice, the dam broke. I couldn't hold back my tears of fear and frustration.

"Sam? What is wrong, are you crying?"

"Heather, I had the police at my house today. I thought I had an intruder but I, I guess I didn't, but now I am holding this necklace, and I do not know where it came from!" The words sounded crazy even to me as they came tumbling out, defying my attempt at coherence.

"What, you had an intruder? You are not making sense, Sam. You had an intruder, but didn't, and now you have a piece of jewelry left by the intruder you did not have?"

"I know it sounds crazy, but I can't explain it over the phone. Will you come over here, please?" I squeezed my eyes shut, not wanting to hear she was too busy or had plans.

"I'm already looking for my keys," she said, then hung up without saying goodbye. This time I didn't care!

I busied myself by getting dressed as I awaited her arrival. When the doorbell rang, I threw the door open and jumped into Heather's arms. I launched into the events of my day without even greeting her or taking her coat.

"I'm so glad you came!" I cried uncontrollably.

"Of course I'd come," Heather said as she peeled me out of her arms. She looked me in the eyes and demanded I get a hold of myself without saying a word.

"I'm sorry to make you drive out here. I didn't know who else to call."

"Sam, what is going on?" Heather looked around while we spoke as if she, too, was looking for my intruder.

"It's in here. I put it back where I'd found it," I wiped my eyes and pointed in the direction of my bathroom.

Heather followed quietly behind as I explained what I thought I'd heard and seen. I entered the bathroom first. My pulse started to rise as I again approached the ornate item. *I will cry 'til I die if it's gone*, I thought. I could almost laugh to think its disappearance seemed worse.

Opening the shower door, I was elated to see it was still there. I turned to show my friend. Heather was no longer at my side.

"Heather!" I called out eagerly.

My stomach flipped as my plea went unanswered. I took notice of the nearby trash bucket, in real fear my last meal might present itself shortly.

"What?" Heather chuckled as she entered the bathroom and came to my side.

"I didn't see where you went," I said with a despondent tone.

"I was just checking around a bit. Boy, I've never seen you so freaked out like this, Sam."

Without a word of rebuttal, I pointed to the necklace that still hung inside my shower stall.

"It's Elvis Presley's, I tell you," I said and handed her the photo book for comparison. "I am *not* losing my mind!"

Heather leaned in to marvel at the piece of jewelry. She seemed hesitant to touch it.

"You can touch it. It's real." I said.

"I don't want to touch it."

"You should touch it and see for yourself." I gave her a little push, desperate for someone to tell me I was not mad.

"Stop that! I said I don't want to touch it."

Her internal brake kicked in and locked her into place. She spun around and exited the shower. Her eyes were big as saucers as she came to rest at my side.

"You're scared of it, too?" I sighed in a hopeless exhale. Heather was the one person I thought wouldn't be intimidated by this predicament.

"I'm not scared of it. We just shouldn't touch it."

We must have looked ridiculous standing side by side, scared of a necklace. I noticed our common stance of hands on hips while judging our dilemma. The beginnings of a smile twitched on Heather's face.

"Sam, there is no way this could belong to Elvis Presley. The man is dead, and I am sure this pendant would belong to his estate by now."

"Obviously, none of this makes sense. But you cannot deny this item is now in my home, can you?" Of all the thoughts careening in my brain, I still kept coming back to the undeniable fact that the very pendant Elvis had owned was in my house.

"Okay, Sam, okay." Heather said in a calming voice. "Let's just sit down for a second and get a hold of ourselves."

She led me back to the kitchen, and we sat down at the table. I found myself once again sitting where I'd been earlier with Mister Iron shuffling papers in front of my face.

I watched as Heather moved with familiarity through the kitchen. When she opened up cabinets and dug out martini glasses, it was as if I was her guest. She began to expertly mix us both a drink. She moved by rote, her mind deeply occupied. For the first time since I'd pulled into my driveway, I checked the time and was shocked to see it was 5:00 p.m.

"Sam, I'll admit that pendant does look like the same one in your book, but the thing we really need to think about is what really has happened. It is more important to consider that you did really have an intruder."

On and on she continued to work the problem out loud, but her words blurred in my ears. Her voice was replaced by Lady Sharone's: *Someone would be sent to help.* My mind locked on those few words.

"Do you remember what Lady Sharone said in Salem? About someone coming to help?"

Heather squinted at me while she ran through her memory. Deep lines of concentration creased her forehead.

"Did she say that someone would come bearing gifts?" She finally said and chuckled.

She approached me with a red concocted martini, expertly not spilling a drop. She placed a glass in front of me and took her normal spot across the table. She cupped her hands around her glass and stared into it.

"Why are you always making booze when we have a crisis?"

It dawned on me that Heather was always the one whipping up a drink after any event, good or bad. I watched her give this serious consideration.

"Bad upbringing?" She joked and took a sip of her concoction.

Her eyes again squinted, this time over the strength of her drink. I looked at my own glass, but could not drink. My stomach was still turning. I was going to have to work slowly at this.

"Maybe it's for the same reason that you are always baking," she offered up as a second thought.

"So, we're back to upbringing then? Well, here's to upbringing." I reached across the table with my beverage in hand and tilted it her direction. Together we toasted with the clink of cheap glass instead of fine crystal, but we didn't care.

My drink was just as strong as Heather's, but I forced it down with great effort. I was keeping a watchful eye out for my disappearing intruder with every sip. Slowly, I relaxed as the alcohol burned its way down. I figured I would either get sick, or I would get drunk and not care. Either way seemed acceptable for the moment. My drink was gone much faster than normal. I got up and headed for the fridge.

"Maybe we should call the police again?" I suggested while digging out eggs and milk.

"You're baking, aren't you?"

Heather laughed and ignored my suggestion. Maybe she wanted to stay on a less upsetting subject. Unsure, I continued to dig out mixing bowls, flour, and all the tools necessary to make something sweet. I relished in the routine of getting ready to prepare something truly satisfying.

"Why don't you just shake your booze, and I'll bake. Then we'll both be happy," I said with my back to Heather's laughing eyes as I set up my working space.

Heather shook a martini mixer with gusto next to me as I fired up my power mixer into the bowl of ingredients. Time mercifully stood still as we set out in our rituals of comfort foods and beverages. Before long, my house was filled with the smell of chocolate and the sound of wobbly women.

"Well, I would say that we sure solved this problem!" Heather said in her slurred, relaxed, what-me-worry voice.

"Yeah, maybe the necklace will just be gone come morning," I offered up while setting two pieces of hot, chocolate-frosted brownies to the table for us to try.

"Oh, I know!" Heather exclaimed just as I stuffed my mouth with chocolate.

"Maybe," she threw a wavering finger my way. "Maybe Elvis will come back and get it."

Heather laughed hysterically as I made a face of exasperation at her. I chewed and swallowed quickly so I could retort, but she was too fast.

"Maybe I should leave." She giggled. "Y'all might want to be alone."

Finally getting my food down, I was too deflated from the alcohol to come up with a good rebuttal. I watched Heather unsteadily shovel a brownie into her mouth. I started to laugh. Fueled by martinis, my laugh grew stronger as lyrics to a song popped into my cloudy head. I realized Heather was now laughing out of sheer compliance. She had no idea what was truly funny.

"If the house is a rockin' . . ." I tried to stop laughing long enough to sing horribly. "Don't bother knockin!"

The comeback, thought witty only because of the alcohol, left me on the edge of my seat in hysterics. Heather's laughter roared. I was sure she had no idea what I was talking about, and that had me laughing even more.

"I am ready for bed. Would you stay with me so I won't be alone?" I teasingly pouted and batted my eyelashes.

I leaned toward the stove to try to see the time, but I found it hard to focus. A combination of high emotions, empty stomach, and strong drinks had taken me to the brink of drunkenness quickly. If I concentrated, the time appeared to be 8:00 p.m. It was early, but the day's stress had bore down on me heavily.

"I figured I would end up doing just that." She smiled and tried to catch her breath from all the laughter.

Standing up with great effort, Heather came around the table to give me a hand. I rested against her for added support for my wobbly legs. Heather guided me out of the kitchen toward my bedroom. My stomach flipped again in torrent of anger over its mistreatment. I pushed back the thoughts of queasiness and concentrated on taking each shuffling step.

"Boy, if my mother could see me now." I said without thinking.

Silence fell over the two of us as we headed down my hallway. My heart suddenly felt heavy, and my soul no longer flew. My words stunned me as I let go of Heather and walked unsteadily on my own. The truth of it was that my mother would be ashamed if she could see me now. My eyes burned from the tears trying to escape my strong hold.

I told myself this extreme emotion was mostly the effects from the alcohol. There was nothing wise in absorbing a depressant into a disheartened spirit. I never have always done the wisest of things in the midst of anguish.

"Sam, you . . ."

"It's okay, girl, forget it. I don't know why I said it." I mumbled as I entered my room and headed straight for the bed.

Heather watched in silence as I struggled to get into my nightgown. I adjusted my pillows and gratefully laid my head down. Once horizontal though, my head spun lightly. I fought to keep my heavy eyes open and pulled up my soft comforter. I looked at Heather and could see the look of hopelessness on her face.

"I'm good," I said.

"Okay. Well, I'm going to go pick up our mess before I retire."

Images of her unsteady hands trying to do dishes brought a slight smile to my face.

"Don't break anything," I said as I rolled over, done with my day.

My bedroom door closed and I drifted off. Though my body was still, my mind refused to rest with me. Instead, it took me back to the dream I'd had in Lady Sharone's sanctuary in Salem. That same distant beeping noise I'd heard while napping on her couch again echoed in my ears. I could smell burning candles and molding books. Once again, I sensed someone was with me. I willed myself to speak, but could not push words from my mouth.

Off in the distance somebody began to sing. I was awash in sweet comforting sounds that tantalized my senses. Slowly, the voice became clearer, and I focused on the deep tones of a man singing. Too quickly, the dream began to evaporate, and I reluctantly opened one eye. Squinting into my bright room, I was surprised to see the morning sun. It streamed through my bedroom window and flowed over my face. Had I not just fallen asleep? I rolled onto my back and lingered in the sun's warmth.

I stretched luxuriously from my fingertips down to my toes and savored the release of tension from my muscles after the previous day. It all seemed so far away, bridged by a delicious dream. I smiled, my eyes closed, and remembered the sound of that sweet singing. It was as clear as though it was coming from the next room. My eyes popped open, and I sat inquisitively up in bed as the fog of sleep fell suddenly away. My friend was fast asleep at my left side. I smiled at her kind gesture of sleeping next to me. I reached over and nudged her awake.

"Heather?" I said in a quiet voice. "Do you hear that?"

Heather slowly opened her eyes. She looked around, not really knowing what she was looking for as she came out of her slumber. I repeated my question.

"Heather, do you hear that music?"

She yawned and wearily rubbed her hands over her face to get her bearings. She looked at me, her mouth partly open for an unasked question. Before she could utter it, a look dawned across her face. Slowly she sat up along side me.

"It sounds like Elvis." I said.

"I know," said Heather as she cocked her head and listened carefully. "I think we should call 911."

"Wait," I stopped her outstretched hand before she could reach the phone. I couldn't bear to go through the events of yesterday again.

My heart raced as I listened to a rich voice that belonged only in heaven. Anything sounding that sweet surely wouldn't bring us harm. I slipped out of bed and casually put on slippers. As I started out the bedroom in sheer determination, Heather stopped me.

"Where are you going? Are you crazy?" She whispered as she grabbed my arm. "We need to call the police, not go out there and wander around with a stranger in your house!"

"Heather, I want to find out what or who is in my house."

Determined to end this craziness, I proceeded down the hallway. Heather was not far behind. The singing was coming from the bathroom. We paused at the closed door.

"It's Elvis' voice alright." I whispered. Confusion began to chip away at my courage.

"Do you have a disc player on?" Heather rationalized.

"Of Elvis singing in the shower?" Once next to the door, I could hear that the shower was running.

"Oh-my-gosh, this is freaking me out!" Heather darted past the bathroom door toward the living room. "I'm calling the police!"

I managed to grab her by the sleeve of her nightgown and pulled her back to me.

"Wait, wait, not yet." I pleaded. "Just go inside with me. I have to see for myself what has been going on in my house."

Heather's unwavering stance told me she wasn't convinced that was a good idea. With the rich sound of Elvis in my ears, and Lady Sharone's vision fresh in my mind, I was going in with or without her.

"Heather, what are the odds that I have an intruder who is an Elvis impersonator *and* who just decides he needs to stop and take a shower?"

The possibilities did suggest this could be something paranormal or even celestial. Though I was slow to accept that likelihood myself, I knew this would give Heather the courage to go with me.

Heather motioned me to wait a moment, then scurried to the hall closet. In seconds, she returned wielding my baseball bat. *Why didn't I think of that*, I asked myself. Much better than the letter opener I wielded myself just yesterday.

I slowly opened the bathroom door. Heather huddled behind me with the bat drawn up. I stopped and took a second to adjust as steam swept over me. I continued, my eyes locked on the shower door. The voice grew stronger as we crept closer. Goose bumps broke out all over my body. The voice suddenly shifted from singing to humming, and we stopped dead in our tracks. I turned to Heather and pressed my finger to my lips. The humming provided us quite a bit less cover, and I was sure our presence would be known soon.

The shower door was at least two inches taller then I. If I were going to see into the stall, I would need to get up close and personal. Scooting up to the door, I pushed myself up close. My heart skipped in terror of giving myself away. I made out a male form through the steamed privacy glass. Heather refused to come any closer. Yet she still held the bat menacingly, waving the end in slow, small circles. I slowly rose, balanced on my toes, and peeked over the top of the shower door.

The man in my shower stood with his back to me, facing the showerhead. I slowly exhaled as my eyes traveled from head to foot. He was tall and lean, with skin the color of caramel candy. I blushed and suddenly felt that I was the intruder as I caught my gaze lingering on his bare backside. The water hit his strong shoulders, ran down his almost feminine but flawless back, and cascaded over his posterior. His body suddenly became rigid, and the slight leg quiver to his own humming stopped. My gaze locked onto his feet. I knew I'd been caught and did not want to look up into his eyes. Slowly, his feet turned slightly in my direction. Time slowed to a crawl. I reluctantly raised my eyes, following a line up his thin leg and perfectly sculpted hip. I continued my slow scan across his chest to the pendant, now nestled comfortably on his body. My vision began to spin, and I lost my tiptoe balance. I had to lean heavily against the door as a crutch. The moist, warm glass door felt soothing on my cheek as I tried to clear my head. I looked over at Heather. Only her enormous eyes moved as she shifted her gaze to some point behind me. Before I could react, I felt a hand encase mine as it gripped the top of the door. A hand with long, shapely fingers rested on top of my taught, white knuckles. In one continuous motion, I jerked my hand away and took too fast of a step backward. I looked up into deep blue eyes that I'd seen a thousand times before in print and film. The scream that had been building deep in my chest since yesterday burst out full force, and I sat back hard on an unwelcoming toilet seat.

"Honey, careful you're going to hurt yourself," he drawled softly. His eyes laughed at me, and I knew that the shower door hid a beautiful, matching smile.

His wet hair changed his look, but those eyes said it all. I knew who he was even without seeing his entire face. In astonishment, I tore my eyes away and turned toward Heather, praying she would confirm my sanity. At almost the same time, we both said it:

"*Elvis Presley?*"

My head was getting light, and I struggled to hang onto my consciousness. With one hand, I reached out blindly to steady myself on the first thing available, which happened to be the toilet paper holder. My lungs felt shrunken and refused to take in the necessary air. As my sight blurred and slowly turned to black, I heard him ask for a towel.

I awoke lying on my couch, feet up, and head on a pillow. Heather sat forlorn across from me on the loveseat. She rocked her body slightly as though in a trance, her eyes fixed beyond me on the far wall. I sat up and chuckled.

"I dreamt Elvis Presley was taking a shower in my bathroom," I said to Heather. My chuckles slowly died as she shook her head from side to side.

"No, it was not Elvis Presley, or no it was not a dream?" I asked. I knew what the answer was when I saw the look of confusion on Heather's face.

"Sam, I do not know what is going on or how this can be, but it does look just like him." She glanced quickly toward the hallway and then back to me.

"Is he still in there?' I asked and snuck a look at the bathroom entrance. Heather affirmed with a nod.

"You passed out, and I couldn't move you by myself, so I grabbed him a towel, and we moved you in here,"

Her words tumbled out almost on top of each other. I paused to digest the curious picture Heather was painting of Elvis in a towel. What might have that looked like? I felt an embarrassing heat rise up from the cold ashes of confusion. Heather's audibly deep breath brought me back from my fantasy.

"I found him some clothes, and he's in there changing now. I swear, I do not know how I stayed conscious," she continued as I sat in stunned silence.

". . . so while I'm putting your feet up, I ask him who he really is, and he says, 'Elvis.' I tell him nice try, but Elvis died damn near 30 years ago. He just smiles at me and says, 'That long?' Then he said something about how time marches on, and wandered back to the bathroom."

"How long have I been out?' I asked, ignoring Heather's reproachful look that I hadn't acknowledged her retelling.

"I don't know, not long I guess." She said and readjusted her position on my over-stuffed loveseat.

"Do you believe he is who he says he is?" I asked, already knowing the answer. I'd just laid eyes on the man who had filled my dreams since childhood. That thought alone had set loose butterflies in wild flight patterns inside my stomach.

We simultaneously jumped when the bathroom door creaked open. Both of us sat straight up and scooted to the edges of our respective seats. His even, steady footsteps finally gave way to the actual man as he entered the room. My vision stayed focused and my head clear as I looked him over in awe and disbelief. Elvis was alive and well in my living room. He was so absolutely, amazingly beautiful. He could have returned to Earth at any age and made a striking impression. However, for whatever celestial reason, the man before us was in the prime years of his adulthood, in his 30s. Those years gave him an air of authority that, in hindsight, I could see was strategic and for my benefit.

As I narrowed my examination, I noticed his hair was not the famous jet-black look for which he was once known for. Rather, his hair was the creamy smooth color of chocolate that God had intended for him, neatly combed back away from his face. He was missing the trademark sideburns. Even in my sad, not-so-baggy gym clothes, he was quite a sight with his hair still wet and his feet bare. I smiled when I noticed the t-shirt he had on was, in fact, Elvis merchandise I had picked up somewhere during my travels. He patiently stood stock still, waiting for us to make the first move. His luminous eyes followed mine to the front of his t-shirt. His perfect lips curled into that heart-melting smirk I'd only seen in photos.

"Who's the funny looking fella?" he quipped good-naturedly.

When we did not respond, his smile slowly faded, and his demeanor changed to that of quiet concern.

"Listen, I know this is scary as hell." He paused, and one eyebrow shot up, as if he shocked himself by cursing. He cleared his throat nervously.

"What I mean is, I am who you think I am." He started to stutter. "Uh, y'all are making me very nervous. Can I sit down?"

Elvis pointed to my recliner and crossed the room without waiting for an invitation. He walked in that easy, smooth swagger specific to Elvis Presley and took his seat.

"I am Elvis Aron Presley."

Hearing him say his full name for the first time snapped me out of my fog. His words still hung in the air as I looked at him, truly seeing him for the first time. I had no idea where to start, but quickly figured where better than the beginning. I calmly took a breath and began.

"My name is Samantha," I pointed to myself. "But, everyone calls me Sam. This is my friend Heather." Heather remained frozen to her seat without acknowledging her introduction. Elvis nodded in both of our directions as he listened.

"I must be dreaming. Or I'm dying" I rested my face in my hands. Good manners dictated that I look him in the eyes, but their depth and beauty distracted me. He waited patiently for me to go on.

"I know you are who you say, but . . ." I struggled to get anything clearly spoken.

I suddenly became very aware that I still had on my nightgown. A slow, unstoppable burn began to work its way up my neck to my face. I tugged on my gown and tried to cover up my bare legs. A smile threatened the corners of Elvis' face as he sat back and watched me squirm in my uneasiness.

"Look mister, you're dead! And you have been since before I was born! The whole world cried for you!" I paused only long enough to gulp air. "People light candles for you every year, on the anniversary of your death. In fact, twice a year, counting your birthday!"

Elvis' eyes grew huge at my outburst. I could not stop the stress of the last two days from flooding forward. Tears began to dam up in the corners of my eyes. I struggled to contain them, desperately not wanting to cry in front of Elvis Presley. Shyly I averted my eyes so he could not see the battle.

He stood up on long, lean legs and crossed the room in only two strides. He joined me on the couch and without asking slid over to be at my side. Caught off guard, I continued to inspect the floor at my feet.

"Are you haunting us?" I asked pathetically.

"Honey," he chuckled as he gently reached to lift my chin, "Is that what you think I am doing?"

I shrunk away from his touch. I needed to put space back between us and removed myself from his side. He leaned forward, elbows on knees, and reached for the pinky finger of his right hand. He had no jewelry to anxiously play with, so his nervous habit would go untamed. He appeared uneasy as he studied the ground below his feet. I instantly felt the need to console him.

"I'm sorry. I'm not usually this emotional." I lied. That's all I had been in the last 24 hours.

"Sam, he is here because of Boston." Heather finally spoke up from across the room, interrupting the extraordinary dance between two unfamiliar partners. We both looked at her questioningly.

"Well, there is some truth to that." Elvis said, looking up. "Lady Sharone is pretty good, but not that good. I was sent by one much more powerful and all-knowing than her."

"Have you been here before?" I asked.

"Uh, a few times." He let out a breath and wrinkled his brow. "I once almost caused a riot at a burger joint."

I never read tabloid newspapers. The media's never-ending quest to hound him, even after his death, was too annoying. The questioning looks on our faces must have told him simplicity was best where this subject was concerned.

"I was hungry. This flesh is weak man, I tell you." He shrugged, keeping it simple and to the point.

Elvis shook his head laughingly. Heather and I looked at one another in astonishment, but neither could find answers in the other.

"Uh, listen ladies," Elvis cleared his throat, "this is a lot to take in at once, I think."

"Are you trying to say that God sent you?" I asked, since Elvis seemed to be expertly avoiding specifics. He only smiled in response.

"Why? What for?" I demanded.

"Honey, we'll have to discover that together. I don't know the plan."

I had a feeling he wasn't telling me all he knew. In total contrast to the reality of the situation unfolding in my own living room, I calmly studied his familiar face—his sculpted nose and high cheekbones. He was as recognizable to me as my very own mirrored reflection. Like an old friend, yet he had been here for only a short time. Already I felt myself taking comfort in his presence, feeling as if I'd known him my whole life.

This God to whom I had not spoken since the passing of my mother had sent someone special down to be with me. My dream, made into flesh, sat only a seat away from me.

Elvis eased back onto the couch to get comfortable. He settled into a slouch that only a man could get away with. He appeared to be observing us as he rested his head on one lone index finger. Only his eyes shifted from side to side, taking it all in. He watched as I fiddled with the edge of my nightgown, then shifted to Heather, who was playing with the soft ends of her long, blonde hair. I could clearly hear my own breathing in the silence that fell over the room.

"Man, ya'll look like a bunch of squirrels," he finally broke our silence. "Ready to scat at any second."

Tickled with himself, he began to laugh. Our unresponsive faces only seemed to tickle him that much more. Soon, he was laughing uproariously. His nose wrinkled in an adorable manner, and he seemed unable to control himself. It was contagious, and soon I felt amused myself. Only Heather appeared unmoved, not finding anything funny. I didn't want to team up against my friend and attempted to hold back my snickering. Elvis tried to calm himself, but the more he tried not to the laugh, the funnier it became to him.

"Oh, mercy," he said in an exasperated chuckle.

"Can you tell whomever plans your arrivals that a shower is not the best way to pop in on someone?" Heather was back to her usual upfront self, saying exactly what she felt. After all, Elvis was not the man of *her* dreams.

"Ah, I'm sorry ladies. It's the uh, little pleasures you miss most." A devilish smile crept over his face. I knew then he'd planned his arrival on his own.

"I, I couldn't resist," he stuttered coyly.

"I know, I know, it was the weakness of the flesh." Heather said impatiently.

"Now you got it!" He teased Heather, nodding his head. God had his hands full with this little angel, I was sure of that.

"Well, I didn't see much. I mean, I'm sure you have enough to see, but I was not trying to see anything. I didn't see anything." *Shut up, shut up!* What was wrong with me? I blushed deeply.

"Honey, I am just glad you peeked before your friend here swung that bat." He shook his head, blowing out a breath between his full lips. "Lord help me, it's gonna be dangerous around here. I can already tell."

The rest of the morning passed awkwardly as each one of us tried to get our own bearings. Elvis did most of the talking and asked questions about our lives. Soon I noticed that none of our answers surprised him. When it was my turn to ask questions, I simply wanted to know why involve our Boston trip, and what would happen from this minute forward. Elvis would not be pinned down. His consistent, firm reply was that he was here to take a journey with me. As for what happened in Salem, he would only say that many people work for The Boss. Some do so unknowingly, as was the case with Lady Sharone.

I had a million things to consider, and time seemed to be wasting away. I came to the reluctant conclusion that if this man was going to be a part of my everyday existence for some unknown period of time, he was going to need to do so in something better than castoff sweats. I was going to have to take the incarnation of the most famous and beloved man in American pop culture clothes shopping. Heather and I put our heads together. Would other people be able to see him? How would we make him inconspicuous in public? He was notoriously hands-on with his wardrobe when he was alive, so how were we to get him to accept today's fashions when he used to set them? Somewhat stumped, we did what all wise women do to back-burner a problem and wait for great answers: we moved back into the kitchen and sat around the chocolate brownies I'd made the night before.

"What do we do now?" I asked.

"Notice we're back in the kitchen," Heather teased, again making fun of my habits.

"Well, its not cocktail hour now, is it?" I threw back playfully, feeling a little self-conscious in front of our guest.

Elvis took a seat with a look of amusement. He watched as the beginnings of a verbal jousting session threatened to kick off. I held back the oral assault I could have laid upon Heather out of bashfulness. The same shyness I'd sworn to overcome in Boston had once again raised its ugly head. I pondered how to overcome it.

"Boy, you ladies sure can put on a show." Elvis expressed offhandedly.

Heather and I came to a halt. We were all ears.

"... especially last night." His eyes widened as he waited for our delayed reaction.

We both turned around to find him smiling at us with a look of playfulness in his eyes.

"That was him." Heather said, as if I hadn't already derived a conclusion.

"Uh-huh. I'm getting that same impression."

I took the seat across from my guest, flipped my hair over my shoulder, and crossed my arms. My shyness began to fade ever so slightly in light of this manipulation. Elvis held my glare as he amusingly nibbled on his bottom lip.

"Unbelievable!" Heather exclaimed and then began laughing. "Rich. This is too rich."

"Seems we've been had," I said to Heather, who normally loves a good game of "burn your neighbor."

Heather laughingly returned to gathering plates and forks. I pulled the lid up off the plastic cake plate that held our treat. All three of us simultaneously inhaled the rich scent.

"You don't get any." My nerves were rattling as I audaciously teased.

Elvis leaned back in his chair. Chuckling, he crossed his arms and mimicked my stubborn posture. His knees bounced stimulatingly under the table. His charm was going to run right over my strong will, and adorable was sure to win.

"Everything was fine, Sam, until you got yourself all worked up and called in the officers." Elvis sighed dramatically.

I melted at the way he used my name in that familiar manner.

"You know, I was really scared," I said truthfully.

"Truce?" His face softened with the first hint of awkwardness I'd seen from him since he'd gotten here.

As he stared into my eyes, I wondered if he knew the power he could easily have over me. I looked away and dished one frosted brownie onto a plate for his enjoyment. It seems poetic now that I shared my one and only comfort food of choice with an angel.

As Heather and I took bites respectably sized for women, we watched Elvis engulf an overwhelming piece of his brownie. He ate with gusto and was not one bit shy. I watched in astonishment. How could I find something erotic about everything he did? I held back my laughter and almost choked on my food. Keeping my eyes on my brownie, I attempted to get a hold of my girlish fascinations.

"This is mighty good, thank you." Elvis sighed contentedly as he wiped his hands on a kitchen towel.

"I do not want to be any more trouble, but I think it would be good to get me a few things. As much as I like this shirt, it's really not me." He smiled proudly as we laughed.

"Yes, well, fifty million Elvis fans can't be wrong." *What a cliché*, I thought as I quoted an old album cover.

He looked up at me and smiled. He seemed to follow my train of thought.

"Well, billions by now, I'm sure," I added and took another small bite of brownie.

"Phew. Billions?" He raised a single eyebrow in question.

"Most likely. But that story will have to wait for another day."

"Impressive," he muttered to nobody in particular.

Unexpectedly, Heather snapped her fingers and excitedly ran out of the room. She returned with her arms piled high with fashion magazines she'd found in my living room. What better way to introduce Elvis to current fashion trends before hitting the stores? Heather and I flanked him at the table and started thumbing through a short stack of magazines. We had his full attention. The midday sun began to warm the room as we tried to narrow down what he would consider wearing. Did he care that the straight-leg pants of the 1950's were a hit In the 80's, but now we were back to the flared pants of the 1970's? Of all the years for him to return during a time of familiar fashion, this was the best. However, keeping things low key would be most important.

"We're going to have to keep things tame," I said.

"Tame?" He said with real confusion.

"That might have been a bad choice of words." I tried to recover. "I just meant we can't attract attention."

"Mmmhmm," he said as he cleared his throat and adjusted in his seat. "Go on."

"There's a saying: 'Only Elvis could pull that outfit off.'" I said.

Elvis' eyes got big as he crossed his arms and looked to Heather for interpretation.

"Sam means that people today consider you a trendsetter for your time, that you had fashion flare," Heather paused to get Elvis' reaction.

"Ladies, ladies, I get it." He held up his hands and smiled. "Let me just say that if I didn't dress in fashion flare, as you put it, I wouldn't have been Elvis Presley. Apparently, I made a lasting impression."

"You underestimate yourself. You wearing a muumuu would have been just fine," I said casually, returning to the magazine I held on the table.

Heather laughed. For the third time that day, I felt my face warm. Elvis smiled sweetly at me as I tried to will myself to shrink inside my own skin. Since crawling under the table would not have been ladylike, I got up and tended to the dishes.

"Ah, why don't I make a suggestion," he finally offered. "Let's just go shopping."

## CHAPTER 3

Shopping is this Southern girl's favorite past time. Shopping with Elvis Presley was going to be another thing all together. The idea of seeing us on the evening news as the object of an "Elvis sighting" in Atlanta was not a pleasant thought. Though he protested, Heather and I persuaded him to wear at least a ball cap and unisex sunglasses for now. Our first obvious order of business had to be to get the man some shoes. "No shirt, no shoes, no business," was strongly enforced in our city.

Elvis seemed to grow a few inches taller in his excitement as we exited the house out into the light of day. The three of us loaded up into my four-seater convertible.

"What kind of car did you say this was?" He asked as he ran his hand along the smooth leather seat.

"It's a BMW." I had to smile as I looked over at him, ready to ride shotgun in the front passenger seat.

"She looks expensive," he said as he turned to me, and his blue eyes briefly fluttered over my white tank top.

I was aware that I possibly fit the stereotypical profile for Elvis' type of woman. As a girl, I had dreamt of having his approval. Now, face to face with his inspection, I was nervous and uncomfortable.

"She's a luxury I allow myself," I said while trying to sound confident and secure. On the outside that may have been true, but on the inside butterflies played rambunctiously in my stomach. My body temperature rose as I clumsily ground the gears in my struggle to find reverse.

"Well, she's a beautiful car," he said as he slipped on borrowed sunglasses and turned his attention away from me. A small smirk crept over his lips.

*Get hold of yourself.* He made me feel like a shy little girl of eight again. After all, he is an angel, not the same man I'd dreamt about my whole life. *He's here for a purpose, a job*, I told myself. Nothing good can come from falling in love with an angel.

"Heather, are you staying for dinner?" I flashed her a look in the rearview mirror. She was too quiet.

"No, I believe I'll head home when we get back."

"But you don't work tomorrow," I reminded her.

"I need to go home tonight. I have something to do."

Heather sounded as if she needed to escape back to her own reality for the evening. I didn't blame her. I was already feeling anxious about being left alone with my guest for the evening.

"What's for dinner, ladies?" Elvis asked. "It's been a long time since I had a good hamburger without causing a riot."

"You're the guest, so hamburgers it is." Heather offered up on my behalf.

I nibbled mindlessly on the ends of my fingernail and thought about what I had at home to whip up in the form of a good burger cook out.

\* \* \*

Few cars graced the parking lot in the one of just many Atlanta malls we chose. We slid into a spot up front near a store that carried men's shoes. Heather and I nervously left our passenger alone and quickly ran in to pick out a pair of size eleven tennis shoes. We returned triumphant to Elvis, but he was not impressed with our pick.

"Sneakers? You pick me out a pair of sneakers?" He chuckled as he looked them over.

"It's all we could get quickly," I shrugged.

He ultimately was a good sport and put them on so we could move on with our mission. As we approached the massive new brick building, I thought how even a person of today's world would find this place overwhelming. We led our guest like a lamb to slaughter through its front doors. Awed by enormity of the mall, he stopped dead in his tracks to take it all in. His eyes traveled upward floor by floor through the atrium to the top fourth level and beyond to the glass ceiling. He was clearly awed.

The perfectly air-conditioned mall welcomed all inside who sought to be shielded from the unusually hot spring day. From the moment of entering, signs vie for the shopper's attention and pocketbook. Eat, drink, and shop away until the end of eternity. Don't worry about spending cash, we take credit cards. Although I loved to shop, sometimes I had to step back and really look at how possession-oriented we're encouraged to be. Sometimes it felt a little wrong to be inside such a modern-day Church of Possessions on a beautiful sunny day. And yet, a day at the mall was a day to look forward to. I sometimes wondered if the families I saw shopping together were really getting the same quality time as if they'd just packed up and gone for a picnic.

Elvis' eyes took in every detail, from the maps to guide shoppers' journeys though the maze to moving walkways, he didn't miss a thing.

"Whew. You have created yourselves quite a little town here."

"You heard of Sunday go to meetin'?" Heather said and added extra twang to her already obvious southern accent. "Well, this is Saturday go to meetin'."

"A store full of over-priced clothes lies straight ahead," I chimed in.

"Follow us, dear sir, and we'll get you looking right proper." Heather swept her arm forward in a grand gesture.

With that, we were off. I realized we'd left our guest behind, so I stopped and turned back. Elvis stood in a comfortable stance with his hands on his hips, weight shifted heavily on his right leg, still looking around at the cavernous mall. I looked around to see if we were attracting any attention. Satisfied that so far we were clear, I held my hands up in question.

"Crazy, they're plum crazy." He said to no one particular as he proceeded to catch up.

How does one shop with Elvis Presley? I had been lead to believe that in his day he would have had this whole store to himself. Shopping off the rack, with all the other animal shoppers, might have been something new for him, but he showed no signs of it. He walked with determination right to the racks, just as if he knew what he wanted. Heather and I watched him pull out a collared, bright blue shirt and hold it up to himself in front of a nearby mirror, then trade it for the same thing in red. After many such rotations of systematic choosing and examining, he had several shirts, a few slacks, and jackets in both formal and casual styles. When he headed to the shoe department while toting all his findings, I began to have some serious concerns.

"Uh, girl, I hope you either have a large balance in your savings account or a credit card. Seems he's on a roll," Heather said with genuine concern as we followed behind him just out of earshot.

"Yeah, seems so. Do you think he's going to try all this on?"

"I don't know, but here comes the cavalry."

Heather nodded toward the two lovely sales ladies headed our way. Shopping in the men's section usually meant sales assistance, this we expected. Judging from the look in their eyes, they were pleased with the manly specimen who had stumbled into their lair for the day. With big hair flying, the blonde and brunette breezed right past us without even a word of recognition.

Our poor lamb never saw it coming.

"Well, hello, darlin'." The blonde reached him first. "My name is Paula. Can I help you set up a dressin' room?"

Then the brunette managed to speak.

"Hi, I'm Darleen. We'd be happy to help you with any alterations that might be needed. Done while you wait, in house, for free," she cooed.

We watched as Elvis turned toward the two women, each eagerly awaiting his response. He smiled that big smile, and his blue eyes blazed.

"Well hello ladies. That would be kind of y'all, thank you."

He seemed elated. We watched the dance from a distance, horrified. The ladies, who were in their early forties, stood at half his height, hair and all. Neither showed any signs of recognition. I could only assume they didn't give him a stereo double-take because they were more likely to be familiar with Garth Brooks than Elvis Presley. They obviously had not been exposed to Elvis' charm until now.

The blonde scurried to scoop up the bundles of clothes while the brunette whisked him away by the elbow to the dressing rooms. As he was being rushed off, he glanced back at us, still smiling big.

I decided that yelling loud enough that customers in the upstairs departments could hear me was the only way to break the spell.

"Excuse me, ladies?! Excuse me!" I screamed.

Both women did an about face, their perfectly dressed heads of hair turning back to us in perfect unison. They stared at us blankly without loosening their grip on either Elvis or the clothes. Neither was sure why loud voices were being directed at them. They clearly did not appreciate the interruption.

I marched up to them in my most authoritative manner.

"Hello. Paula and Darleen, is it?" I said. "Ladies, exactly where are you hauling off my fiancé?"

I could tell by the wide-eyed look on Elvis' face that he was as surprised as the hair twins were about our engagement. Our lovely ladies looked as if I'd just taken their only bottle of hair spray away from them. Their eyes narrowed and faces darkened with frowns. Without shifting their stares, they each dropped their death-grip grasp on their victim. Elvis rubbed his arms and watched with a bemused look. It was a standoff as all of us ladies sized each other up. I looked Paula, the blonde, up and down, and figured she out-weighed me by at least thirty pounds. This would get ugly if she got too riled. I was going to have to play it cool but confidant. Elvis moved away from his captors and took his place by my side. He slid his arm around my waist and drew me close.

"Sorry, honey, didn't mean to ignore you." He laid a soft kiss on my cheek. "These nice ladies were just helping me find a dressing room. Ladies, meet Samantha."

He gave me a little squeeze. For just a moment, all I could think of was the spot his lips had just touched.

"I just wanted to be sure you weren't getting kidnapped, dear, never to be seen again." I laughed. The hairspray twins exchanged glances and followed suit.

All five of us continued the walk to the dressing rooms. Heather and I pulled up a few comfortable chairs that were normally reserved for tag-along men and waited for the runway show to begin. Paula and Darleen hovered behind us. We all gazed appreciatively at the transformation from the handsome guy in gym sweats who went in to the cover-model who came out. We sucked in and held our breath as he paraded by in a black jacket, off-set with a bright blue shirt and black slacks. We could not speak. Elvis stood nervously and waited for opinions.

"Ladies?" He pleaded for one of us to give him something. His eyes were wide, arms out, almost begging someone to speak. Heather and I snapped to attention first.

"Yes. Very good. Uh-huh. Yup," Heather managed.

"Great. Nice, looks good," I agreed.

"Oh, nice, sir. Yes, looks very good on you." Paula stated.

"Oh!" Darleen gasped.

Paula suddenly stepped forward and brandished a small measuring tape. I like to think she kept it tucked up in that big stack of hair.

"Sir, we could measure your inseam there and see if it might need to be taken up a bit or let out some?"

I shot her an incinerating look. Paula met my gaze and quickly averted her eyes.

"Or, not." She stuttered. "Actually, I think it looks like it'll work as is."

"Oh!" Said poor Darleen, still unable to gather herself.

Paula reached over and smartly slapped her arm. Darleen glanced around in confusion, not sure what was going on around her. I just couldn't believe this man still had this effect on the opposite sex.

Elvis turned away from us gawking women to admire himself in the mirror. It appeared as if he liked what he saw, though he made no comments out loud. Rather, he kept adjusting his collar and tugging at the cuffs of his shirt, but his wide smile of acceptance gave him away.

It's amazing what a riot a good-looking man can cause. Other women started to drift over to see what the noise was all about. Like metal to a magnet, the fact the crowd was growing only drew in more curious onlookers. Heather and I knew without conferring that we needed to shut this fashion show down. We quickly gathered up all the clothes Elvis wanted and tried to make an escape. Getting him to leave the store without just one more little thing was harder than dragging a child out of a candy store. He complicated our efforts by chatting randomly with other shoppers, seemingly oblivious to all of the "haven't-I-seen-you-somewhere-before" stares. I swore I even heard a few ladies make mention of how the nice gentlemen looked an awful a lot like that dead singer. Maybe I imagined the comments, and maybe I didn't, but the situation was getting much too hot for my comfort. I threw my final thanks over my shoulder to the clerk at the register as we nearly ran out of the store.

"Man, that was fun!" Elvis beamed breathlessly as he settled back into the car.

Heather and I wiped the sweat from our brows and each sighed a breath of relief.

"Do you not realize we almost caused a riot?" I made no effort to keep the exasperation from my voice.

"Oh, the ladies were only having some fun."

"They were about ready to attack! Also, I swear to you some were trying to figure out where they'd seen you before." I looked around us in the parking lot as I fired up the car.

"Those ladies were as nuts as my mother on a red-tag sale day!" Heather chimed in.

"That's it. We're going to die your hair!" I said.

"Die my hair!"

"Yes. It's got to be lighter or something not as Elvis-like." I imagined what he might look like as a blonde and remembered that he had been in one of his movies.

"'Elvis-like'?" He repeated disbelievingly.

"Well, some people don't even know he ever had brown hair." Heather said in his defense. "Maybe we could leave it, and he could wear hats a lot."

"I like black," he stated matter-of-factly.

"Listen, you're known for a lot of things now, and black hair is one of them! Black is out, so what is left?" I tried to reason.

"Maybe we should trim those side burns down a bit more too, just in case," Heather offered.

We both examined his profile closely.

"Oh, now girls, let's not get carried away here," he chuckled.

"Oh, yeah. They're in, but they're out . . ." Heather started to explain.

"I know, let me guess. Too Elvisy? Well, honey, I've been down this road before. Bring on the clippers!" Elvis had to accept that we could not be reasoned with.

We made small talk all the way through the heavy Atlanta traffic, back to the safety of home. As I looked over at him, I realized it had been along time since I had felt so alive. *Why had God sent this man to me?* I wondered as my thoughts drifted to what the link could be. *Why would God take something so dear from me, like my mother, and then send something so unusual in her place?* I suddenly realized how quiet everyone had gotten. I glanced at Elvis, and our eyes locked in a light friendly gaze. He winked at me, and I smiled back easily before he turned his attention back to Heather for another round of questioning.

*Maybe coloring his hair blonde was a tad extreme*, I thought. After all, nobody had ever had the chance to see a middle-aged Elvis with light brown hair. He sure did look especially handsome and fresh in his younger days. However, much could be said for that Greek-god like appearance that dark hair had given him then. My mind lingered on how black offset his smoldering blue eyes. Those eyes were always the first thing I noticed in every photo taken of him. *Well almost everything, let us not forget that butt*, I reminded myself. A new round of blushing started as I considered how truly sexy he was. I snuck a quick glance his direction and found he was already again smiling that all-knowing smile. My eyes grew wide with the fearful thought that maybe he knew what I'd been thinking. How was I to know what angels could or couldn't do? Turning my attention back to the road, I tried to assure myself he didn't have such powers.

"U-hum," Elvis cleared his throat and sat with a closed fist resting over his mouth.

"What? Did you say something?" My heart raced as I watched him cover up his smile.

"No, honey. Didn't you?" Elvis put down his hand to show me an all too serious face.

"No. I, I didn't say anything."

I tried to calm myself for real fear I might pass out while driving. I could see a questioning look on Heather's face in my rearview mirror. She was lost in the conversation.

"No? Okay, then." He turned back around and gazed out his window while smiling lightly.

*He can read my mind! Oh shoot, I can't stop!* Every cell in my body wanted to scream. I had to convince myself I was mistaken. He was just laughing at my obvious childhood torch blazing bright as the burning of Atlanta in *Gone With the Wind*. When would this ridiculous little girl go away and my true grown self get back in control? *Obviously not during this car ride*, I thought as I pulled into my driveway, exasperated with my out-of-control position.

\* \* \*

Evening time is a favored time down south. One can finally escape the never-relenting sun that shines almost daily during the summer. In my neighborhood, every evening like clockwork people venture out from their air-conditioned sanctuaries into a sun that's finally setting. Voices rise over the rhythmic creak of porch swings, and the grills are lit. Friendly debates volley over backyard fences as to which neighbor has the better barbeque sauce. To this day, my daddy's grilled burgers remain famous in the neighborhood where I grew up. One of the few gestures my father made that resisted my rebellion was to hand down the fine art of a good ole barbeque. Just the smell of hickory or mesquite chips can bring back a flood of good memories. Over the years, the simple act of preparing food had become a way for me to relax. On that first night with my guest, there was nothing more I wanted to do then cook up some burgers. Maybe this would allow me to collect my feelings and settle my mind.

I pulled into my driveway and closed the car's convertible roof as Elvis and Heather unloaded bags from the trunk. The smell of lit grills was already heavy in the air, and the sun was still an hour from setting.

Elvis held the front door open for me and Heather to pass through. I smiled happily as he affirmed what I'd always read. He was a Southern gentleman to the core. We were only home a few moments before Heather was gathering herself together to leave. She pulled me aside for the pep talk she felt I needed.

"Okay, Sam, I've got to go now. Just relax and remember, he's just a man," she said, then added, "For the moment, anyway."

We both looked to see if he could hear us. He was busy in the kitchen. Our words were safe.

"That's what I'm afraid of." I lowered my voice so that only she could hear. "I don't have the strength to deny him anything!"

"My gosh, girl. Get a hold of yourself!" Heather exclaimed in a low tone. "He's an angel!"

"Yes, he is." I said, as my eyes glassed over.

"Oh, you're helpless!" Heather said as she headed for the door.

And just like that, the angel and I were all alone.

The silence of the house magnified the awkwardness of our situation. My senses were on a razor's edge. I busied myself opening a bottle of wine and took a long, grateful sip from my just half-full glass. Elvis was not a drinker during his lifetime. I assumed the same held true for him as an angel and was not surprised when he kindly declined.

"I can turn on some music for you while I get the grill started," I offered as I watched him take his newly bought suit jacket off to lay it across my recliner.

"Alright."

My eyes lingered on his stunning blue shirt, now in high competition with his eyes. I turned my head shyly and tried not to stare. Casually he took a seat on my couch. His legs set wide apart and comfortable, he watched me as I headed for the stereo.

"Do you want to choose a disc to listen to? Or, we can just turn the radio on and scan for something you like." I said.

He looked past me at the jumbled array of electronics stacked in the entertainment center.

"Why don't you pick something for me honey and then come sit down here for a moment." He patted the spot vacant next to him.

"Okay." I could feel the alcohol rushing through my veins, but that relaxed feeling had not come over me yet.

Not wanting to make my guest feel uncomfortable, I picked out some music from his era. The musical changes from the last thirty years seemed like a subject too immense to approach in what was left of our day. I chose a disc and handed it to him, then put another into the player. He inspected it from all sides.

"Amazing, man." He shook his head. "All that music on this little disc."

"Is this all new to you? Or does The Boss keep y'all up to date with the technology?"

"We hear about things." Elvis said.

Ray Charles' smooth, melancholy voice filled the house, and I felt a little of my stress finally melt away. Even as a child, when I couldn't live up to the high standards set for children of pastors, I would hide within a world full of music. This world lived just inside my bedroom sanctuary. I would sit for hours and play records over and over again. Though on this night, I could never have imagined I'd be face to face with my artist of choice. Unbeknownst to him, his voice had comforted me many nights until I fell fast asleep. I started to tell him that but stopped short. This night already felt dangerous without me potentially adding fuel. Maybe he was already aware of how many people would love to thank him for that same comfort he had given to them on a lonely night.

"That is beautiful. Sam, come sit here with me." Elvis patted the empty spot next to him and shook me from my trance.

"I probably should go get started on those burgers," I said as I fiddled with my glass.

"That can wait a moment. Come on, honey," he cooed. "It's just ol' Elvis here. I don't bite."

I had all but gotten comfortable with the idea that a wildly famous, long-dead icon was essentially living with me—that is, until he said his own name. He spoke in that butter-melts-in-his-mouth way, and I responded like a woman with no willpower. Sure, I walked over and sat down in the most casual way I could muster, but my heart was galloping at anything but a casual pace.

"Well, sir. I don't know you very well, but I'll make an exception this time."

I was rewarded with an innocent smile that oozed charm as I sat down next to him. He turned to face me.

"Oh, you know me," he said and reached out to take my unsteady hand.

"I do?" I could barely hear what must have been my own voice over the pounding in my ears. I focused on his long slim fingers as they engulfed my small hand.

"Uh-huh. And I know you."

"How do you know me?" I asked and started to pull my hand away. He gently tightened his grip.

"I've been with you," he paused before clarifying. "From time to time."

"With me?" *What was he talking about?*

"Uh-huh". He shifted so his whole body faced me, and my captured hand disappeared inside his two.

"I see." I said, but I really didn't. How could I possibly decipher whatever he was trying to tell me while he held my hand?

"I miss this." He said softy, briefly distracted. "Holding a beautiful woman's hand, I mean."

"How long have you been with me?" I asked shyly.

"Since your mama passed, Sam," he said quietly and released my hand with a pat.

This was the first mention of my mother since his arrival. I flashed back to all the times as a child when she would tell me how God sent guardian angels to protect or comfort us when we needed it. She used to say these angels could be family members who had passed or strangers picked by God himself for a special purpose. I remembered lying in my bed wondering who my guardian angel might be. Never would I have guessed it could be Elvis Presley.

"You're my angel?"

"Yes, honey. Surprise," he said and smiled sweetly.

Despite the new round of questions forming in my head, I smiled at him. Thoughts of private moments that he probably had seen swarmed in my head. Surely, there was some privacy in this world? I could only assure myself that was the case. The alternative was too unthinkable to consider.

"I'm not trying to scare you, Sam." He leaned into my view to force me to look at him. "You said earlier that you felt as if you've known me since you were a little girl, and I thought it might help to know that I'm familiar with you, too."

Elvis sat back and eyed me expectantly. I should have reacted somehow, shouted, cursed, cried in happiness or fear, but nothing came. I had stretched and met my emotional limit. It's not every day one meets their guardian angel. I fell back on what was safe, familiar, and required no conscious effort.

"I think I should go tend to the burgers now, or else we'll be ordering take-out as a last resort."

I rose and quickly headed for the patio door and left my guest alone with Ray Charles singing 'bout that woman who had done him wrong.

Once outside, I walked barefoot across the soft grass. As I approached the grill, I relished in a sun that was now much lower in an early evening sky. Purple and pink graced the skyline as the sun slowly descended for the day. I smiled at its beauty as I mixed my daddy's special spices into the meat with my bare hands. The mixture was cold between my fingers. I mindlessly molded the patties and threw them onto a hot grill. Steam blew up into the sky. I watched as the burgers turned from blood red to a warm brown without really seeing any of it. Memories of my father flooded my mind as I stood motionless in front of the grill. I remembered how my mother had told me Daddy had always wanted a boy. However, never questioning God's choice, I was told he was thrilled when I arrived.

With all that had happened during the last twenty-four hours, and who knew what chaos was before me, I found myself thinking about how long it had been since I'd seen my father. It was odd how I could still love him so much and yet so easily avoid his sporadic phone calls. The day my mother died, he became the human, tangible extension of God—the very God who had cause the deepest heartache of my life. For years now I'd been unable to fathom how daddy could preach about and even worship this God who had stolen his wife and my mother. Now I find this same God has been watching over me, caring enough to send a beautiful angel to be with me on Earth.

I stared at the hot coals as they erupted into bursts of flames under the dripping burgers. I let the rising heat wash over me as my thoughts came back full circle to the present. Looking down, I contemplated the new splatters that decorated my already well-worn apron and watched them rise and fall with my deep, even breaths. I had no more energy left, no more fight. The anger I'd actively fed and kept alive for years suddenly felt week and small. In its place was a sliver of happiness, something I had not felt in so long that I was scarcely able to recognize it. I glanced back at the house and was happy to see my angel had not followed me outside. I was grateful for my few moments alone. As I laid out dinner on the patio table, I heard the music pause from inside. I hesitated, then soon heard another tune begin to flow out from within my house. Elvis had put on Elvis. I smiled widely at this newly re-mastered rendition of an oldie-but-goodie.

"Amazing what they can do with sound these days," he said as he stepped out of the house and inhaled, flashing an easy grin. "Hmm, something smells great."

"Thank you. That would be the burgers."

"Man, it's so clear. It jumps out at ya," he said while heading my way, still excited about the music

"This is an alternate take." I hesitated, almost forgetting to whom I was really speaking. "I believe."

"Well, that part I'm not sure I like. Releasing my unwanted takes and all," he straddled the bench and sat down at the picnic table.

"Yes, well, the demand is high without you here. They do want to please your public."

"Ah, yes, that was always important."

He began to load up the burger I'd placed in front of him and considered the condiments around the table. I'd always heard the man could eat; now I was going to see first hand.

"Do the fans like it?" He looked up at me expectantly.

"Yes, well, we love anything new." I smiled, surprised how calm I was considering my passion for the subject.

He took huge bites of his burger, but his eyes never left mine. He could gaze into my eyes longer then anyone I'd ever seen. Although his silence was warranted by a mouthful of food, it still made me uncomfortable. My dinner cooled while I scrambled to keep conversation going.

"Well, personally, I'm grateful for the efforts made to find unheard material. I was not yet born when you, uh, passed." It struck me what a strange thing that was to say so casually.

He continued to watch me closely as he loaded a mound of potato salad onto his plate. Avoiding his eyes, I thought in amusement that for once my obsessive grocery shopping was paying off. Had Heather stayed, she would have had a joke to offer right about now, I was sure.

"Are you my number one fan, honey?"

I was shaken out of my thoughts by his sudden question. Words stumbled around in my head, but nothing acceptable seemed to present itself.

"You're okay," I said. I cleared my throat and tried to play it cool.

"Just okay?" He said suspiciously as he scanned my face for the truth.

"Yep. Just okay," I repeated and reached for a burger of my own.

A cricket struck up a tune somewhere in the background as the world seemed to stand still for the day. Elvis sat silent and watched my every move. I tried to ignore his intense stare and continued to spread dressing over the burger bun. Daring to glance up, I only briefly saw the grin that lingered around the edges of those sweet lips.

"Well, I guess that's all one can hope for," he sighed, sounding very let down. "You know, being gone so long and all."

I told myself he was only trying to get me to crack, but he seemed so disappointed. I began to feel awful for kidding with him so horribly.

"Alright." I put my burger down, thinking maybe I've gone too far. "Me and millions of others are your number one fans."

His face perked up with my admission. He straightened up in his chair, leaned on his elbows, and gave me his full attention. His intense stare and posture compelled me to continue.

"When I was a kid, I had photos of you all over my room, even on the ceiling! My family thought I needed serious help." I stopped when I saw him smirk.

"Did you now?" His face abruptly changed to sympathetic understanding, and he seemingly hung on my every word. Whoever said he wasn't a good actor should have seen this.

"You're pulling my chain, aren't you?"

"No." A straight look of innocence washed over his face. How many looks can one man have?

"Yes, you are!" I laughed, embarrassed. I got up to go into the house where I could eat in private.

"Wait, wait, Sam. You're just so cute when you get frustrated. Come here and sit back down now, I'll behave. Don't leave, honey." Laughing, he jumped up and caught me by the arm.

He tugged me back, sat me in my chair, and took his seat across the table from me, still chuckling.

"It's not funny!"

"Okay, okay. Man, you *are* feisty!"

My breath caught in my chest at such a simple comment. It sounded to me as if he had been told that very fact and by someone who had first-hand knowledge.

"Who told you *that*?" I asked.

He looked at me as if he had let out some secret that wasn't to be mentioned.

"My mother, did she tell you I was feisty? Have you seen her?" The emotional roller coaster fired up again. I knew it wouldn't take much on this track to make me cry. Elvis' face was unreadable, as he looked me in the eye.

"Sam, that was said off the cuff, honey. That's all it was."

"What, The Boss doesn't want you telling me?" My pulse quickened. A game of tease was turning serious for me.

"No, that's not . . ."

"You get to see your mama every day?" My words choked over my emotion.

Elvis' eyes quickly flashed in anger at my challenging words, only to then soften into a look of compassion. Those beautiful blue pools, now riveted in confusion, would not meet my heated stare. Though I was aware he'd lost his mother while he was alive and knew the pain I was going through, to me, it was my pain alone. He stood with me as I rose to collect my plate.

"I think I need to excuse myself." I turned to leave and ignored his hands-on-hips stance of a man losing the battle and maybe even the war.

"Sam," he said softly. "Please."

I was unwilling to hear more. I quickly walked inside as tears ran down my face and splashed into my plate of untouched food. I just let them flow. After all, I'd grown accustomed to their company. They were like old familiar friends, these tears of grief.

"The guest room is the second door down the hall, on the left." I threw over my shoulder without looking back.

I left him outside alone that night with the smell of fresh-cut grass drifting over from a neighbor's yard. He didn't try to follow me, and deep down I wished he would have.

* * *

When I was a little girl, my daddy used to say that God could hear his children from anywhere. If a child was not sure what to say out loud, they should write it down, and God will read it. Because of those fatherly words, I had been keeping a journal from the time I could write. That night, alone in my room, I finally picked up that journal that had been collecting dust upon my nightstand. I brushed my hand over its familiar, worn leather edges and opened to my last entry. It was dated two years ago, the day we laid my mother to rest.

*Dear Diary,*

*As a little girl, I knew when I put words to paper, somehow they were taken up to you on angel's wings. This knowledge always made me feel special. Today, I don't feel special. Instead, I feel alone and abandoned. Where are you? Why are you not coming down here to make everything right again? You ignore my prayers and my tears. Why should I spend any more time on you?*

I closed my diary and slowly slid it back to its rightful spot where it could collect more dust. I wiped away my last tear for the night with the back of my hand and stretched out on my bed. Rich singing floated through my open bedroom window. Elvis was still in the back yard where

I'd left him. His voice sounded sorrowful as it tugged at my heart.

*"Oh, Danny boy, the pipes, the pipes are calling,
From glen to glen, and a down the mountainside.
The summers are gone, and all the flowers are dying."*

Expertly he controlled his voice as it rose and fell between the notes smoothly and without strain. His singing could still make me smile when I didn't feel like smiling. Just as he'd always done in the past, he gave me comfort. One by one, my tense muscles loosened, and the ache between my shoulders began to subside. Sleep was a warm welcome to my tired soul. Soon I drifted far away. That smooth rhythmic beep, now present in all my dreams, awaited me.

The morning sun soon washed across my bed in cheerful greeting. Unwilling to acknowledge its warmth on my face, I rolled over and let it envelope my back. I arched myself into a luxurious stretch. My mind lingered comfortably in that not-quite-awake state of bliss. The warmth from behind gradually turned hot and forced me into the present. I reluctantly began to replay in my mind the events from the previous night. My heart sunk as I remembered the words that had caused that spark of anger on Elvis' face. The scene played repeatedly, refusing to be ignored even after I opened my eyes. I rolled onto my back and listened hard over the ruffling sheets. I judged from the sounds of gentle creaking floorboards in the hall, my houseguest was up.

Did angels even sleep? So far, he seemed to feel and do everything a mortal man might do. He ate food and displayed the simplest of human emotion straight from his eyes. I assumed from his comments the night before that he found some pleasure simply in holding my hand. He appeared to be as much a man as he had ever been.

The sun was really beginning to beat upon me. I finally pulled myself out of bed and crossed the room to close the blinds. It was going to be another unusually hot spring day, and I hesitated to even consider that summer was fast approaching. The sun was acceptable for the moment, but soon it would become my enemy. I cringed at the thought of what life must have been like before those wonderful cooling units were invented.

I stepped out of bed and into my private bathroom. Very aware of the man in my house, I planned to quickly move through my morning routine. As I eased into the warm water, I imagined all my tension from last night washing down the drain beneath my feet. Out of the shower faster than normal, I was soon primping in front of a mirror. I deftly pinned my hair up off my neck to help stay cool and moved on to expertly apply my makeup.

I giggled like a schoolgirl as I pulled my favored yellow sundress from the closet. Boston had been too cold, but wearing it today would make up for that. I smiled knowingly as I slipped it on. The sunflower yellow complemented my lightly tanned skin. The dress fit snugly at my waist. I sat at my grandmother's tiny vanity and savored the final step of my routine. I crossed one long leg over the other and rubbed in body lotion. The sweet familiar scent of lavender filled the room as I worked the lotion over my tiny feet and up my calf. Satisfied that I was presentable, I slipped on a pair of one-inch heeled sandals and walked out into the hallway to look for signs of life.

From the hallway I could see into my cluttered office through the partially opened door. The same rustling noises I'd heard while in bed were now clearly coming from that room. Elvis had wandered into my private world, a world in which until now he had unknowingly been a part.

My heart leaped as I remembered the first Elvis record my mother had bought me. We had sat on my bed one summer afternoon and listened to the record while Daddy was busy at the church. Mother understood my fascination with Elvis and regularly took my side in disagreements that got loud enough for me to hear over the records I played endlessly in my room. To Daddy, it reeked of idol worship. Only as an adult did I realize he must have worried about how it looked to his congregation.

I held in a chuckle as I heard a stack of records shift and slide like a deck of stiff, new cards. Elvis swore softly. I paused before entering the room. He was in the one sacred place I kept as a reminder of those special childhood days. Some of the mementos that I'd hung in my own home were the same ones I'd hung when I was only eight years old. It occurred to me how strange it must feel to him to be the subject of my little shrine.

I tiptoed over the creaky floorboards to the doorway and peeked in unnoticed. Elvis sat at my desk, fully dressed and ready for the day in beige slacks and a collared red shirt. He was engrossed in a magazine article that I had labeled and cataloged in the "1990s" decade notebook. I quietly watched his profile. His eyes squinted as he read. After a moment, his eyes no longer moved across the lines but focused on some unidentified point. He stared as if lost in a thought, his perfect features blank. Suddenly, he rose and walked to the window just behind him. His abrupt movement made me jump out of my skin, and I tried to slide out of view without catching his attention. I waited until I heard him move back to the desk and continue his inspection of my memorabilia. Unsure of his mood, I peeked around the doorway again. I was relieved to see he looked calm and curious, like anyone else who has seen my collection for the first time. I knocked on the door to give him fair warning.

"Good morning." I said, hoping he wasn't upset with me for last night.

"Sam, you're up. I, ah, got restless and was just looking around. I hope I didn't intrude. I, I wasn't aware of what was in here." He smiled at me but would not meet my eyes.

"Relax." I smiled so he wouldn't know how unsettling this scene was for me. "I would think you might feel more uncomfortable in here than I do."

"Why's that?" He cocked his head and rested both hands on his hips.

"I'd imagine seeing your face all over a closed-up room would be a little unsettling, to say the least." I laughed nervously.

"Well, it is like being in a room full of mirrors. But I've seen my face in just about every place imaginable. This is tame, sweetheart." He shook his head and chuckled.

"I suppose you have." I marveled at how he put me at ease.

"But, one thing does bother me." He took a step toward me and smiled devilishly. "Why's my face only in here? I looked around this whole house, and I don't see me anywhere else."

I looked around the room to stall but could not come up with a good answer.

"I guess I prefer you in private." I tried to shrug casually, but then made a hasty exit as his mouth dropped open.

His laughter echoed out of the office and followed me tauntingly all the way into the kitchen. The preprogrammed coffee machine had already done its morning drip, and I headed right for it. I filled a cup and snuggled it in my cold hands as I sat down at the table. The distant sound of the office door closing and approaching footsteps made me straighten in my chair.

Elvis sat down across from me and cleared his throat. I waited for a retort to my suggestive comment, but thankfully none came. It was a relief to find I could be comfortable just being myself around him now.

"You look very pretty this morning, Sam." He scanned my attire in smiling approval and held out his hand. I felt obliged to take it.

"Well, thank you, kind sir. Let me say you look right fetching yourself," I gushed while keeping my eyes lowered.

I looked up as he released my hand and settled back in the chair. He looked down smiling, his lips curled into a smirk at my attempt at a complement. His chipper demeanor told me all was forgotten from last night's emotional outburst. This was a new day, and I was done trying to figure out why all this was happening. After all, there were worse things in life than spending time with a dashingly handsome man, especially one whom I believed had enough electricity to light up the city of New York.

# CHAPTER 4

It is my humble opinion that the city of Atlanta, Georgia, offers visitors the best of fast- and slow-paced worlds. Downtown is alive with buildings that rise imperiously toward the sky, chic stores that boast the trendiest clothes and housewares, and restaurants that are known equally for fashionable food and patrons. Atlanta will completely satisfy a taste for modern, bustling city life. When the senses have reached overload from the sights, smells, and sounds of a big city at full tilt, the historic district offers a much slower, quieter refuge. Even as a resident who knows the area inside and out, I still love the majestic antebellum homes with their classic white columns found in the older parts of town. I think every tourist who sees the area is looking for his or her own Tara.

Occasionally a new business does pop up in this part of town, but its success hinges on fitting in amongst old and established merchants is a difficult task. A few months before I met my angel, a coffee house with new-world features nestled into this mature neighborhood. The interior was decorated in an upscale style with large dark-chocolate colored recliners. I loved the atmosphere the first time I walked in. It was thick with comfort and rich with the scent of leather. Long gone are the hard, wooden chairs and impersonal furnishings of establishments of yesteryear.

With only the promise of something new to experience, I loaded up Elvis in the car and headed out that day with the top down. Graceful old live oak trees lined the streets on both sides of my neighborhood. Elvis resembled a classic mobster in his dark shaded sunglasses. He looked up appreciatively at the ancient, intertwined branches that formed a tunnel over our heads. As though he'd never seen them before, he studied each one in turn as we cruised through.

I gently wound down through my car's expertly engineered gears and pulled into The Colonial Coffee House parking lot. Two older gentlemen in their 70s sat outside at tables shaded from the Atlanta sun. I imagined they'd been there all morning sharing stories of a time long past. As I shut off the car and gathered my purse, Elvis stepped out and stretched. He'd been folding and unfolding his long legs in and out of my cozy car for more then a day now. I watched as he slid his dark sunglasses down his nose and leaned in towards the shop's floor-to-ceiling front windows. Just inside sat a group of young women in the comfortably cool interior, clustered around a small table barely large enough to hold all of their designer coffees. The girls waved, and Elvis smiled lazily and waved back.

"This way, Prince Charming," I joked as I walked in between Elvis and the giggling girls.

Today I was going to introduce Elvis Presley to the technology of my generation. I had always fantasized what great fun he would have had chatting in real time with his fans online. I was sure he would have appreciated the activity if it had been available to him in the 1970s. After watching him in deep thought earlier this morning in my "shrine room," I decided I'd show him a little of what he'd left behind.

"This is a new spot, but in an old part of town." I said while waiting for him to catch up. "I've got something to show you that I think you'll find interesting."

"We're going to have some fun today, are we?"

"Well, who knows how long you'll be here. I decided this morning we weren't going to waste any more time."

Elvis pulled open the door, and I stepped by him, close enough that I could have given in to impulse and kissed his delicious cheek. The smell of fresh-ground and brewed coffee beans hung heavily in the cool air. I watched Elvis' face as he read the overhead board and began to comprehend that each one of the choices was solely for a coffee drink. His mind must have been reeling, I mused. Gone were the days of ordering a 10-cent cup of joe. Today, a person has to make actual decisions: plain coffee, flavored coffee, espresso, a latte? Or maybe a combination, a white chocolate café latte mocha? Skim or whole? With whip? To go or to stay?

This shop had it all, which is why I liked it so much. I walked straight for the counter with my choice in mind. Elvis lingered behind me. When I turned to ask him what he'd like, he was still stalled in the entrance. I smiled at the clerk behind the counter as I took a step back to help coax Elvis along. The girls by the window giggled and whispered in each other's ears.

"Are you coming?' I asked Elvis, who was still taking it all in.

"This is a coffee joint?" He asked innocently.

"Yes. Well, by today's definition anyway. Come on, you don't have to order anything complicated if you don't want to." I motioned him to follow my lead. "Just ask for regular coffee."

The clerk, who looked to be a college student, tapped his pen on the cash register impatiently. Elvis stood behind me with his hands on his hips, still flirting with the young girls at the window like a teenage boy. *I can't take him anywhere*, I thought as I heard him clear his throat and get back into our situation at hand.

"Hi. Sorry. I'll have a medium white café mocha, no whip and skim, please." I turned to Elvis and smiled so he'd know how easy it was.

The young man wrote my order onto an empty cup and turned to Elvis. I lightly nudged him

"Just a small coffee. Thanks."

The young man waited and looked expectantly at Elvis, who nervously cleared his throat.

"Uh, black?" Elvis asked.

He bit his lower lip, and I knew he was trying not to laugh. The young man started to write down Elvis' order of black coffee onto the cup in his hand.

"Hot." Elvis added suddenly.

The girls' laughter erupted behind us. Elvis looked back at the young ladies and laughed with them. He had an audience. He looked back at me as I rubbed my temple, shrugged his shoulders, and tried to contain himself. How could I resist such a good sense of humor? As long as he was willing to laugh at himself, I could not help but join in.

The young man paused to see what all the ruckus was about. Elvis leaned over the counter to see if the young man was writing it all down.

"I like it hot," Elvis repeated in between his breaths of laughter.

The clerk held the cup so that Elvis couldn't see and mimicked writing "hot." He then looked over the cup at us with a withering look and turned away to start our orders. I slapped Elvis' arm in a playful manner.

"Ouch," he laughed. "What?"

"You are crazy, aren't you?" I asked. I walked to the opposite end of the counter to wait for our order. Elvis followed me, still laughing softly.

"So I've been told, baby."

Our order was done a few minutes later. The same sullen young man slid the cups across the counter toward me. I thanked him sincerely and hoped he hadn't done anything regrettable to our drinks while his back was to us. I made a mental note to talk to Elvis about the dangers of teasing wait staff before the order is served.

"Thank you," Elvis said over my shoulder, still amused. The young man walked back to the register without responding. I suspected he'd had his fill of characters for the day.

Elvis dutifully followed me to the back of the shop. I purposefully directed us away from the distraction of staring young women and instead sat him down facing a computer monitor. He glanced at a customer who was engrossed in an Internet search three machines down. Elvis followed suit and moved the mouse around in front of him. He smiled broadly as the screen bloomed from a dead black to a bright blue home page.

"Fantastic," he said.

I gave him a two-minute crash course introduction to the Internet, careful not to dwell too much on what it was, but rather what it could do. I was pretty sure our surfing neighbor was a cyber geek, and I wasn't about to get technical within his earshot. An expert I was not.

"This is amazing, I'll give you that," said Elvis as he drank in both coffee and technology. I was impressed at what a fast study he was.

"Want to see what happens when you type in your name?" I tossed out the bait and wasn't surprised when he took it.

"My name?"

He hesitated, then moved over so I could slide in next to him. My chair scooted easily, and I ended up sitting close enough to him that our legs touched. I was instantly focused on the contact and nearly melted when he pressed his leg more firmly against mine in a cozy manner.

"This is nice," he said softly.

He was close enough to tickle my ear with his warm breath. The giggling from the front of the shop had stopped, and out of the corner of my eye I could see the girls watching us.

"Hmm?"

As much as I enjoyed the flirting and how often it seemed to be happening, I could not get over feeling conflicted every single time. *He is an angel*, I tried to remind myself. I could not go on feeling weak at the knees every time he got inside my comfort zone.

"Mr. Presley," I said in a low tone and turned to look him eye-to-eye. "I think you're just a big flirt. Does your boss know you do this on company time?"

The slow rise of pink in his face was answer enough for me. This was a turn of events, and I felt powerful at the idea that I could make Elvis Presley blush like a schoolboy.

"Sam, what exactly did you bring me here to show me?" He teased without moving.

"I brought you to show you this here computer." I accepted his challenge and did not move my body or my eyes from his.

My leg was getting very warm and not just from contact, but from contact with a man who I could barely resist on my strongest day. I could feel his leg trembling slightly. *Am I making him nervous?* The realization that I was getting the upper hand in our little game made me feel something close to heady euphoria.

"You smell awful sweet from here, honey. What perfume are you wearing today?"

He was trying to take back control. Elvis closed the last few inches we had between us and leaned into the nape of my neck as if to get a better smell. His lips felt like fire as they lightly brushed my skin in an airy kiss.

"I, I don't remember." That he made me lose a little bit of my control vaguely irritated me.

Elvis broke away first. He straightened up in his chair and chuckled low so as to not disturb the other patrons. The girls near the window laughed in my direction. I shot them a look hot enough to disintegrate them and their cheap knock-off designer jeans.

"So, what did you say you want to show me?"

I tried to refocus and remember what I was going to show him before he turned perfume analyzer.

"Don't remember? Well, we can always go back to what we were doing," he teased as he started to move in again.

I threw up my hand between us and turned my head away. He sat back and sighed deeply. This man could stir feelings in me in a way no other man I'd ever known could, no matter how long I'd known them. It almost frightened me sometimes how fast I was falling for someone I was just really getting to know.

I cleared my throat, straightened my chair, and readjusted the screen so we could both see it. I gave the mouse a shake to again bring the computer screen to life. Elvis' face lit up with it.

We spent the next hour surfing about subjects that interested him. First, it was football. He was excited to see that Tennessee had a team in the National Football League now.

"Look, you can watch clips from past games, too." I said as clicked on a video link.

"The Titans, huh? Well, it's about time," he said as he pressed his lips together in consideration.

After what was probably far too many coffee drinks and making so much noise that all other cyber customers left, I finally remembered the real reason why I'd taken him there. I asked Elvis if he wanted to see what he had become.

"You're going to show me what I've become on this here gadget."

He ran his hand over his mouth, puzzled with my offer. Without waiting for his approval, I typed "Elvis Presley" into the search box and set it loose. In one second the screen filled with hit after hit. I scrolled slowly down the page so he could see the list with the tally of total hits at the bottom. The number was astronomical.

"16,900,000, to be exact," I said.

He stared open-mouthed at the screen. I clicked on a well-known site. The screen flashed as it reloaded, then up came his image. A lovely photo of Elvis doing what he did best danced across the site's home page. A music file fired up while graphics flashed and banners blazed. I backed out of that page and clicked on the next link, then the next, until we'd gone through the first page of hits.

"A fan can come here and listen to your music if they want. Or, they can watch a video clip of you." With the click of a mouse, I brought up a clip of Elvis swinging a dance move in "Live a Little, Love a Little."

Music blared from the computer's speakers as I cued the song "Edge of Reality." Elvis frowned and frantically looked around for a way to silence it.

"Where's the plug to this thing?" He shouted at me over the music.

I quickly closed the video. The room went silent again. A sarcastic "thank you" came from our friend behind the front counter.

"What are you doing, Sam? Are you tryin' to give me an upset stomach? Whew, mercy." He shook his head in disgust. I tried not to laugh.

"There are concert clips in here, too, if you'd like to see them." I leaned forward toward the mouse. Elvis grabbed my hand.

"Honey, you're going to stress me out. There's only so much me I can handle." He was laughing, but I was sure he had seriously had enough.

"Sorry, I can get excited playing in . . ."

"Here, take that dilly and hit that," he interrupted with a sudden request.

I didn't want to ask what a "dilly" was, so I was fortunate he had his finger on it for my direction. My eyes widened as I read the word "chat."

"Chat? You want to go to a chat room?"

"Why not? It's gotta be better than the 'Edge Of Reality'." He laughed at his own joke.

Elvis paid close attention as I chose the chat link. Immediately, a box came up and words popped in from fans who already were busy sharing stories. Elvis silently looked at me with absolute wonder.

I logged him onto the chat site and made his handle Angel35. He watched as Angel35 popped up and waited for someone to give it words. I pushed the keyboard over in front of him.

"Angel35?" He asked. "That's me?"

"Yup. You did want to chat, right?" I pointed at the dialogue still scrolling in the background.

He watched as lines of conversation cascaded onto the screen in rapid-fire succession. Every other sentence held his name. He was the reason they were there.

"These are my . . ." He stared at the screen, either unable or unwilling to finish his train of thought.

"That's right. These are your fans," I finished for him.

Before he could continue, his fans unknowingly welcomed their hero into their conversation.

Tigerman: Welcome Angel35.

Heartbrkhtl: Hello Angel35.

Nmbronefan: You're new. Big E fan are you?

I looked at him and waited for him to say something. I tapped on the keyboard in his hands. He could only look down at it, lost in thought. He positioned his hands and began to pluck awkwardly at the keys. With what very little typing talent he could muster, Elvis reached out to his audience for the first time in nearly thirty years. Tears began to well in my eyes as his face again lit up with excitement. Only the sparkle in his eyes outshined the lopsided grin that was fixed on his face. I resisted the urge to take out my camera phone to freeze him in time.

Angel35: Hello. Thanks. Sure, I'm a big fan.

He smirked at me and shrugged his shoulders. I patted him lightly to encourage him to continue.

Tigerman: Ah a new fan! Keep the up and coming generation tuned in I always say.

Angel35: No, I'm not a new fan. This is my first time on a computer though.

I watched Elvis try to get acquainted. They shared with him how he had touched their lives. The stories were familiar to me—some even could have been my own. Many in the chat room felt a special kinship to him, having grown up in the 1950's when teenagers didn't have a voice. Elvis came along and became the representative of an entire generation. Some grew up on his music because of a family member who had been a fan from the beginning. Some cultivated their love for him from a parent who passed it on. Others told stories of lonely times in their lives when his music had given them hope. Every single one had his or her own story, but all of them had something special tucked away in their hearts that he'd given them through his talent.

Angel35: He never imagined how this would continue for so long after he left.

Elvis typed slowly and was careful with his wording. Any careless slip could cause mass confusion and upset a delicate balance, so he methodically pecked out each entry.

Tigerman: No, he was a humble man. It wasn't in his nature to think such a thing.

Heartbrkhtl: Exactly! He underestimated his influence on people's lives.

Nmbronefan: I just wish that his fame wouldn't have been such a burden to carry. In the end, it seemed as if it was.

I watched Elvis consider all that had been said before he typed his next line. His eyes never wavered from the screen, and his hands shook every so lightly as he tried to convey his feelings.

> Angel35: Rest assured he felt privileged, even in the end.
>
> Nmbronefan: I wish we could have helped him in some way.
>
> Heartbrkhtl: Most didn't realize what was happening. Maybe our love for him was too distracting?

Elvis smiled. His eyes filled with emotion as he read and then waited for an opening to speak.

> Angel35: God's will was done on that final day. I guess he tried to be superman. Turned out he was only just a man. Imagine his surprise?

As if all were actually in the same physical room to feel the emotion, the cyber chat stopped. I held back my own tears, but they were tears of joy, not sorrow. As elated as I felt for Elvis to have this experience, I also felt a pang of guilt that I had let down my fellow fans by keeping his true identity a secret.

> Angel35: He would want everyone to know how grateful he was for all the love showered onto him all those years.

A few seconds passed with no response. I imagined all were wondering who was this Angel35.

> Angel35: I'm sure he's eternally thankful.

Tigerman:     Angel35, where are you from? You talk as
              if you may have known him.

Heartbrkhtl:  Ya, I was just going to say that.

For the first time since connecting with his public, he looked at me. I wondered how far was he going to take this conversation. His hesitation and the raw look on his face told me this act was hard for him to maintain.

Tigerman:     Angel35, are you with us still?

"Be careful," I warned him. "Their devotion has no end, and they'll quiz you if they become suspicious."
"I would like to tell them." He sniffed deeply, then steadied himself. "To let them say goodbye."
I softly smiled and spoke carefully. I needed to reach his head, but would have to do so through his heart.
"We all said goodbye a long time ago. We know how you felt."
His slight smile told me he understood. *We can't go back.*

Angel35:      No, I didn't know him.

Nmbronefan:   He made you feel as if he was your friend.
              Not sure if he knew that or not.

Angel35:      I'm sure he does, now.

Elvis sat back and crossed his arms as he tipped back in his chair at a risky angle. A bus boy cleaned tables nearby and paused to look at us like we were nuts. I didn't care. When Elvis met my gaze, I knew I was looking at a man who was at peace.
"There was a time when being "Elvis Presley" felt too heavy for one man to bear alone," he said before pausing. "But now, it's all right."

I was rewarded with that famous grin that could light up a room.

"What else ya got?" As quickly as that, he changed the subject.

We left the shop and climbed back into my car. Elvis waved at the girls, who still sat at the table by the window. They had long since stopped their giggling and were probably completely unsure what to think of this man now.

"They probably think I'm nuts," he said and turned to me with a laugh as he worked vigorously on a stick of gum.

"You are!"

He nodded in agreement. I pulled back on to the main road and drove onward to our next destination. The sun was still high in the sky, and it felt like the kind of day where time would treat us kindly. We drove in thoughtful silence for a bit until I pulled down the last side street that would lead us to the freeway. I shifted into high gear and merged from the entrance into traffic. I had decided to show Elvis my favorite place in the world: the family cabin on Carter's Lake.

My daddy had bought this quaint cabin back in 1985. The waves on Carter's Lake bordered several miles of fine beach property, all covered in sand that was the color of caramel candy. As a child, I could barely wait to dive into its warm surface. I would kick my shoes off first thing upon arriving and run straight for the beach. My mother's pleas for me to not get my pants dirty always fell on deaf ears.

Spectacular countryside that grows more beautiful with every mile flanks the road north out of Atlanta. Once outside of the city's evil web of freeways and skyrocketing buildings, the Blue Ridge Mountains make a starting contrast. The mountains spread across 3,000 acres of forest land that is painted with a touch of maple leaves and stark pine boughs. Turn after turn, the hillsides roll alongside soft and welcoming. My father often used to say that the drive alone out to the lake was a religious experience.

After a while, I turned off the main highway onto a paved road that led into the mountains. I knew it as a short cut. In all my years of driving this way, I had never seen but a hand full of cars on it at the same time. I took one last turn before pulling onto the shoulder so we could get out. I stretched my legs and took in the deep scent of Georgia's famous, forest-grown wild ginseng. The only sounds were the soft idle of the car engine and the rustling of maple leaves in the light wind.

"Where you goin'?" Elvis asked as he watched me walk around to his side of the car. I flung open his door and motioned for him to get out.

"This is the only place I could think of where a man like you could drive in private." I smiled and waited for it to sink in.

"Hot damn!"

In one smooth motion, he jumped out of his side and slid into the driver's seat. I had never been good at being a passenger, especially after my adventure with Heather, and figured now wasn't the time to sit quietly. While he got buckled and adjusted, I issued instructions.

"Okay, this road goes on for at least 30 miles. There are many sharp turns, and it winds around pretty dramatically at times..."

He took a moment to study the lights and meters on the dashboard, completely oblivious to anything I said. Elvis turned to look at me. His eyes were well hidden behind his dark glasses. His face suddenly broke into an enormous grin. I tightened my seatbelt.

"Hang on!" He yelled and clenched his teeth in anticipation of the thrill.

The car lurched forward and threw back road dust as Elvis dropped it into gear. I scrambled to get my sunglasses back on before the wind blew them off the top of my head.

My car was mechanical perfection and handled with precision. Elvis drove like a professional—despite the sometimes knuckle-whitening rates of speed, he was always careful and in control. He chomped obsessively on his gum as he took the winding corners with ease and used the gears to get through them. I'd had the car for some time, but the truth was that I'd never had a better time riding in it. As we zipped through another set of curves, I caught sight of a parked car in my peripheral site. I almost gave myself whiplash as we flashed by, and I spun in my seat to get a better look. What were the odds that in all the years I had spent time on this road, today would be the day a sheriff was on patrol? He must have been out for a nap before we blazed through his moment of serenity. His lights flashed on as the patrol car jumped out into the road behind us.

"Oh, Lord help us!" I screamed over the wind.

"My thoughts exactly," Elvis hollered back.

"I can't believe our luck!"

Elvis pulled the car over at the first wide spot in the road, and we waited for the sheriff to catch up. I tried to use those few seconds to form a plan.

"Okay, okay, listen." I rambled. "When he comes up, tell him you lost your driver's license. He'll give you a ticket, and we'll leave. Okay?"

"Okay," Elvis said as he took out his gum and placed it in the ashtray.

"He'll want an insurance card, and it's in your visor. The registration is in the glove compartment. Just tell him it's my car," I continued, trying to cover all bases.

"Relax, honey. I've been pulled over before. I doubt it's changed much."

His words still rang in my ears as the sheriff pulled in behind us. He stepped out in a cloud of dust and strode to the driver's side of my car. As he got closer, I looked twice at his familiar face. My mouth dropped open, and I said in a voice that I did not recognize:

"Oh ... my ... God."

The words came out of my mouth in slow motion, like in a bad dream.

I felt Elvis' eyes rest on me the same way my daddy's used to when I'd taken the Lord's name in vain. I turned back around to face the windshield and covered my face in my hands. Just as the officer stepped up to the window, Elvis finally turned.

There he stood, one of Atlanta's finest, in a fully pressed and perfect uniform. The only item on him that was out of place was the Elvis-style sunglasses that rested on his slim, pointy nose. I couldn't stop staring at them, as I was sure they were not standard uniform attire. His long, obviously died jet-black hair hung out from under his sheriff's hat. I swallowed hard as I noticed a set of extra long side burns on a face that was quickly approaching retirement age.

"You're sure in an awful big hurry there, young fella. License and registration, please," he drawled.

Worry began to set in as I watched Elvis be subdued to an unrecognizable point. He took off his sunglasses and folded them into his hand. I carefully leaned forward to look around Elvis and get a better look at our deputy. Sheriff John Paul, said his shiny, perfectly straight badge. He stared sternly into the car while awaiting some response to his request. He clearly took his job seriously.

"Listen here, son. I'm going to need your driver's license." Sheriff Paul repeated testily.

I reached over and touched Elvis' shoulder to help bring him back down to Earth.

"Uh, yes. Yes, sir." Elvis said and pretended to reach for his wallet. His hands actually shook just the slightest bit as he fumbled in one pocket after the other.

"I, ah, don't seem to have it, sir."

Sheriff Paul stopped writing in his ticket book and paused for effect.

"I must have left it at the house officer, I'm sorry," Elvis continued.

"I see," the sheriff said in displeasure.

He slowly reached up to take off his glasses and silently inspected them. The heat of midday Atlanta beaded up on his forehead.

"Well, son, that's a problem." He never lifted his eyes from his glasses as he reached into his back pocket and pulled out a bright white, neatly folded handkerchief to wipe the dust away.

"See, in these parts, that's illegal," he droned.

Sheriff Paul finally made eye contact with his subject for the first time. As their eyes met, a fleeting look of surprise passed across his otherwise stoic face. He blinked questioningly at Elvis, and his composure seemed to crack. Slowly, the sheriff's head tilted to one side, much like the family dog. He seemed to let minutes pass before speaking. I wondered if he wouldn't just pass out.

"What's your name, son?"

*Name?* We hadn't time to discus what his name would be. My heart jumped up a notch, and I held my breath.

"Jon Burrows," Elvis said as he casually put his sunglasses back on. He threw me a quick smile that I desperately hoped the sheriff hadn't caught.

It was as if I heard the name in slow motion. Serious fear gripped my fast-beating heart. The sheriff's eyebrows shot toward the sky and settled right back down until his eyes were tiny slits. His hulking, stocky body descended upon my convertible and into Elvis' face.

"Boy, I don't know what's going on here, but your joke is not taken kindly."

Elvis' mouth hung open, but no words came forth. He rocketed from self-assured and witty to completely confused in a split second.

"Sir, I don't understand," Elvis pleaded. "I mean no disrespect, and I'm not making a joke of any kind."

Sheriff John Paul nearly blocked out the sun as he stood tall over Elvis to study him. He unexpectedly turned to me.

"Ma'am, your ID, please. Or is yours at home, too?"

"No, sir. This is my car." I quickly shuffled through my purse and handed over my license and registration. I hoped I could restore credibility to the situation.

"Sir, he is who he says. We could bring his ID to prove it when we pay the ticket."

The sheriff broke his glare at me to shift it to Elvis, who smiled his big grin. I cringed and silently willed him to stop trying to be charming. His attempts were not well received and only seemed to fuel matters. The sheriff did not smile back.

"Remain in your car," he ordered and strode back to his vehicle.

We watched the sheriff return to his car with all my information in hand. He was barely out of earshot before Elvis started in.

"What in the world was that all about?"

"'Jon Burrows'?" I stage whispered. "You couldn't think of something new?"

"Sorry, it was the first name that came to my mind. I wasn't aware it was so connected to me."

"He thinks you're making fun of him."

"Well, I don't recall having that long of sideburns," he joked.

"This isn't going well. He probably assumes we're mocking him, and that won't be good for us."

"Well, I think he's a rather handsome fellow." Elvis looked back over his shoulder and waved at the sheriff, who was comfortably seated in his air-conditioned cruiser.

"You're making it worse." I slapped his arm. He was compounding the situation, but I couldn't help but laugh just a little. His childishness could be catching, in spite of the serious matter at hand.

"Well, he is," Elvis chuckled.

"Real funny. He thinks you are trying to look like . . . well, *him*. Now some kind of game will start."

"Him who? Oh, like H-I-M." He said and rubbed his chin pensively.

Elvis leaned toward the rearview mirror and slid his glasses down the bridge of his nose. He peeked over the rims and feigned shock.

"Hot damn, I am him!"

"Fine." I said, trying not to laugh. "I'm not helping you now. Get out of this by yourself."

I crossed my arms and turned away to look out of my side of the car. Although I'm well known for my stubborn nature, curiosity got the better of me after only a few seconds, and I turned back toward Elvis. To my irritation, he was already facing me and grinning, just waiting for me to cave. I gave up being the adult and stuck out my tongue. He laughed delightedly.

"Relax, honey. You say there's a bond amongst my fans? So that means he and I have something in common: me." He patted me reassuringly on the arm

"Well, start bonding, because here he comes," I whispered.

The sheriff's mood appeared not to have improved as he resumed his stiff authoritative stance next to my car.

"Mr. Burrows," he said with obvious annoyance. "What is your street address?"

I had reached over Elvis to retrieve my ID from the sheriff's barely extended hand, and dropped everything in Elvis' lap to try to buy time before he answered.

"Sir, that would be Memphis, Tennessee," he said snickering as he picked up my mess.

"What?" The sheriff and I spoke simultaneously like a couple of mynah birds.

"Uh . . ." Elvis stammered as if he was unaware of what he'd just said. "Sir, I mean no disrespect. I can see you're a big fan of Elvis Presley's, and so was my mama."

He stole a glance my way that said, "How am I doing?" I just held my breath.

"You see, sir, my mama named me after him in that strange round-about way."

Up until that moment, I would never have guessed an angel could lie so convincingly. I wondered if God considered it a hazard of the job he was conducting.

"I see." The sheriff adjusted his squeaky leather gun belt and put his sunglasses back on. "Well, son, your mama sounds like a genuine fan."

"Oh, yes sir, the biggest I'd ever had. Uh no, what I mean is, the biggest he'd ever had." Elvis smiled big and proud for the law.

"Yes, well, I'm sure." The sheriff seemed touched, but had to regain his control of the situation. "You will need to let this little lady drive, as you don't have your license handy. Meanwhile, I will be writing you a ticket for speeding and driving without your license."

"Not a problem, officer. Seems I'll be in Atlanta for awhile longer. This pretty lady isn't getting rid of me quite yet." He took my hand in his, lowered his glasses, and winked at the sheriff.

The sheriff smiled a thin, knowing smile and nodded, man to man. I looked from our entwined hands to Elvis' face. He flashed me a grin. *So this is what losing your mind feels like*, I thought.

"My boy, my boy," Elvis said as he turned back toward the sheriff.

What passed for a chuckle slipped from the sheriff and blended with Elvis' outright laughter. I blushed deeply and wished I could melt right into my butter-soft leather seat.

"You young'uns stay safe now, and slow down."

Only on a movie set could Sheriff John Paul have made a better exit. He touched his hat in a parting gesture and walked back to his cruiser. The late afternoon sun filtered through the dust his tall boots kicked up. Not until he pulled a u-turn and drove away did I finally relax. Elvis still held my hand.

"'My boy, my boy'?" I asked sarcastically.

"What?" He laughed.

"I'm sure I read somewhere that means something," I said accusingly and squinted at him while I tried to drum up an old memory.

"You shouldn't believe everything you read Sam," he replied as he gave my hand a loving squeeze before parting.

We again switched seats and continued on our drive. I made some short stops along the way so we could take in the scenic views of the lake. At our last stop, my favorite lookout point, I could see the sun was going to be down soon. We only lingered for a few moments to enjoy the shadowy blue water as the sun sparkled upon it.

We soon came to the gravel driveway that led to my parent's cabin. I realized it had been two years since I'd been there. I remembered how after I was out on my own, mother and I would come up for girls-only weekends. We'd sit on the porch in rocking chairs and watch the sun come down over the lake. Our conversations were always light, and she would laugh at the stories I'd share about the ever-so-colorful traveling public.

As we drew closer to the cabin, I was surprised to see the driveway looked as though it hadn't been tended to in a long time. Rain had dug out holes large enough to do damage to a small car like mine. The grass on either side of the driveway was tall and dead. I couldn't imagine my daddy would leave this place in such bad shape. Judging by the condition of this road, he hadn't been up here in a long while.

"Sam?" Elvis said. I don't know how long we'd been sitting in the driveway idling.

"Hmm?" I looked at him and slowly refocused. "Oh, sorry. I was just trying to remember how long it's been since I've been here. I hope the place is still standing. By the looks of this road, that might be a stretch."

I carefully guided my beautiful car between the many deep potholes. The cabin was barely visible through the overgrown brush, just around another bend. As we arrived, I thought it looked even more dark and alone in the woods than it had when I was young. The windows were boarded up, and the cedar siding had faded. Too many years of harsh weather and neglect had dimmed the warm light-caramel siding to a cold gray. Needles and leaves obscured its rooftop. Without getting out of the car, we paused briefly to assess the sad state of the tiny, two-bedroom cabin that hosted some of the best days and nights of my childhood. I hoped the lake wouldn't betray me as well as we continued past the cabin.

"That was it?" Elvis asked as we passed by.

"Yes, but nobody's been up here for some time." I said simply. "The lake is beautiful, and it's down just a bit further."

My heart lifted as the lake came into view. It was just as beautiful and inviting as when I ran toward it as a child. I smiled and remembered how I barely took time to throw down my towel someplace dry before splashing headlong into its mild, clear depths. The lake was so large the opposite side couldn't be distinguished clearly with the naked eye. The light breeze smelled fresh as it pushed wave after wave up on the tan sand. Small picnic tables made by the locals sat on grassy knolls about every hundred yards. Today they sat empty, but with summer approaching, soon they would be full of families and freshly made food.

I parked the car, and we got out without a word. I dropped my sunglasses onto the driver's seat and strolled toward the nearest picnic table. The sun was just starting to go to bed for the day. Its rays bounced off the lake and left little diamonds of light that danced on the water's surface.

"My daddy used to say those were God's diamonds out there," I said and pointed as I took a seat.

Elvis only smiled and sat down next to me. We sat quietly and just watched the wind play in the trees and on the water. I closed my eyes and took even, deep breaths. Why had I waited so long to visit this place again?

"Is heaven as beautiful as this?" I asked without opening my eyes. I must have interrupted his own contemplation, as he paused to collect his thoughts before speaking.

"More."

I turned to look at him. He had removed his sunglasses and placed them in his shirt pocket. I marveled at how the warm light of the sun caressed his face. Its reflections sparkled off his blue eyes and made them seem of a softer blue.

"Why come back, then? And why come back for me?" I asked.

"Because it's beautiful down here, too. And, I miss the simple things that maybe I took for granted the first time around. Like this lake here, and the smell of these trees." His face was peaceful as he spoke.

He lifted his head into the wind and closed his eyes, and a grin played across his face. I realized I hadn't smelled the trees and flowers until he'd mentioned it. I took a deep breath and savored the smell of jasmine that must have been growing somewhere nearby.

"And . . ." he looked back to me and seemed to think a moment, ". . . the touch of another human being."

Elvis took my hand into his and lifted it to his lips. He kissed my hand ever so softly and then rested it upon his knee. I was startled but resisted the urge to move as he leaned slowly toward me and stopped just a few inches from my face. He smiled again as he gave me a moment to adjust.

"Do you mind?" He asked with an innocent smile. He didn't bother to wait for the answer I was never going to give. Our lips touched ever so softly and all too briefly.

". . . and kissing a beautiful woman."

His sweet breath was warm on my skin as he pulled back to speak. He lingered within inches of my lips. I marveled at how long his eyelashes were as he studied my mouth. Fearful of breaking the moment, I held my breath and hoped with all my heart he'd kiss me again. Suddenly, he sat up straight. He cleared his throat and scooted a few extra inches away. The high I had been riding crashed hard, and I wondered what I had done wrong. Elvis stared straight ahead at the lake and offered no explanation. My heart pounded heavily as we sat in silence.

In my lifetime, I had never felt such electricity from another human being's touch. My body tingled from head to toe as my temperature rose to an uncomfortable level. I stole a look at him and was surprised to see his face was flush with emotion, too. Yet, he sat quiet and still, seemingly unreachable. I felt the sides of my face with shaking hands. Heat radiated from my face and burned into my palms, and my lips still tingled from his kiss.

"Feels wonderful, doesn't it?" He turned toward me. I felt transparent in his gaze, as though trying to hide anything would be useless.

"Did you just make that happen?" I asked. Maybe angels have some powers over mere mortal humans. He only smiled at my naiveté.

"No, darlin'. We made that happen."

He scooted back next to me and took away my loneliness. He curled a strong arm around my back to my waist and brought me to him tightly. I rested my head upon his chest, right over his racing heart.

"You're such a baby girl," he said in a childlike tone and kissed me lightly on the top of my head. My heart skipped as I heard him use that loving title from my past.

"My mama and daddy call me that," I said. "Baby girl."

"I know. I like pet names," he said as he rested his head upon mine.

"You didn't answer my other question." I stalled for time, unsure of how to handle myself respectably in such close contact with him. "Why me? I still don't understand."

"I know you don't, baby girl. We don't get to choose who we're sent to watch over, Sam. But your loved ones are always with you, honey." He brushed my hair out of my face with his free hand

Elvis leaned away from me and lifted my chin up so I could look at him.

"Always."

He watched the tears well up in my eyes. I knew that I didn't have to explain they weren't tears of sadness, but of joy. I was happy because I believed him and because I felt loved while with him.

"I've always loved you, you know? Even though we'd never met, and I was just a little a girl . . ." I felt relief in saying it. His eyes were yielding as he examined my face, only inches away from his own.

"I know," he murmured tenderly.

My heart pounded as I looked into his eyes and saw a raging storm inside their depths. He gently held my chin with his trembling hand and lightly brushed his thumb across my lips.

"You're so very beautiful, Sam."

My lips quivered in anticipation as he reclaimed them as his own. His kiss was tender and lingering at first. My head began to spin, and I lost myself in the moment. I never wanted it to end. Suddenly, his kiss turned from gentle and slow to eager and urgent. He pressed his body deeper against mine. I moaned with pleasure as his tongue passed over my parted lips and danced against mine. A jolt ran to my spin and sent waves of passion through my entire body. I ran my fingers all the way through his hair. Just as I thought he might claim my very soul, his kisses became ever so gentle once more. Slowly, he sampled my mouth. His hot breath quickened against my skin.

He began to pull away. Unwilling to break our union, I kept my mouth pressed to his and followed his lean. He gently separated us, then sat upright and took controlled, even breaths. I noticed his hands trembling as he ran them through his now tousled hair. He brushed the back of his hand lightly over his lips and moved over smoothly. I stared silently at him, but inside I screamed for him to just look at me, to say something, anything. I tried not to believe he'd play with my feelings like this. There had to be a reason for this sudden change of atmosphere. He just sat with his gaze fixed on some unknown point out on the water, now dark and inky in deep dusk. He shook his head. I felt myself near tears yet again as I imagined the worst of what he must be thinking. I knew he'd felt the same overwhelming electricity and wanting that I had. Yet, he appeared disheartened. I looked down at my tightly clenched hands and tried to corral my hurt feelings. After a few minutes, he finally turned back to face me. Without thinking, I pouted in the way that always worked on my daddy. Elvis started to chuckle and sat up a little straighter.

"No pouting now, baby girl." He rubbed his face with both of his hands and shook them out at his side. "Phew, Lord have mercy."

Elvis turned back to the lake and began to softly laugh to himself. He seemed to be struggling with his emotions. I didn't want to give him time to regain his control and better judgment. I started to scoot closer to him.

"Uh-huh. You keep yourself over there, woman."

Elvis laughed nervously and slid off the picnic table to stand in front of me. Ever conscience of his appearance, he ran his hands down his thighs to smooth his pants. In the near darkness, I hoped he didn't notice my eyes following his movements. I couldn't help but fantasize about what could have just happened on that table. I abruptly averted my eyes when he cleared his throat.

"We better get now, before we both get into trouble." He pointed one finger at me, then pointed two fingers to his own eyes. I got the message.

He turned on his boot heel and began to walk back to the car alone. I watched him walk in smooth Elvis fashion. His arms hung far out from his sides. My eyes fluttered down his strong arms to his delicious behind. With each long stride on those slim legs, his pants curved and pulled taught. *Oh girl, you'd better get a hold of yourself!* I turned away and ran a hand through my own hair. I stood up and straightened my favorite yellow dress. As I walked toward the car, Elvis' silhouette was visible in the passenger seat. Though it was almost dark, he had placed his sunglasses back over his eyes.

We drove in silence. Each of us was absorbed in our own thoughts and unwilling to discus what had just happened back at the lake. Instead, I thought about the drive itself and how it always seemed so much faster to go home from the lake. I wondered if it was a holdover from when I was a child. The ride out to the lake seemed to take all day. My daddy used to get stern with me when I urged him to go faster just one too many times. The noticeably cooler night air swirled around our heads and helped me to think clearly. I turned on the music. Unable to bear the silence any longer, I tried to explain the multitude of channels that make up satellite radio. As I took our exit off the freeway, I punched up an all-Elvis station that I knew well.

"You have your own channel, by the way," I said casually.

Elvis finally took off his glasses as his own voice bounced out from my stereo system.

"It just keeps on getting better." He said and smiled playfully.

As I made the last turn of our journey and headed down my street, my stomached rumbled commandingly. I suddenly realized just how long it had been since I'd eaten.

"I'm starved." I watched him as he fiddled with the radio, surfing different channels.

"I could eat," he said absently.

"You know, there's a local band that plays not far from my house. The lead singer and I went to school together, and this place has great food."

"Really?" He continued to push buttons. "What kind of music do they play?"

"Everything really, but mostly they play the blues."

"Well, let's go." He sat back, satisfied with the channel he'd found.

"I need to freshen up a bit first, if you don't mind."

I was really telling him, rather than asking. We had been out all day, most of it in a convertible. To freshen up sounded wonderful to me. Though I loved my yellow dress, I was ready to put it back in the closet for the day.

"Whatever you say, little lady," said Elvis as he pointed straight ahead, as if to say "drive on."

\* \* \*

I truly enjoy the process of getting ready for a night out. I love to make a whole event of it. I set the ambiance by turning on music and lighting candles. I might even enjoy some wine as I put on makeup and style my hair. This night however, time seemed precious. I skipped much of my cherished routine and was ready as quickly as I possibly could be.

I was like a teenager again as I struggled to pick out something to wear. Humming along, I flipped through the large wardrobe I'd been adding to for years. Each seductive garment was considered, and the undesirables were discarded on the floor. The knowledge that earlier in the day I'd had some affect on Elvis the man made my choice that much more important.

I finally spotted a black dress suitable for the evening and pulled it down from the hanger. In front of the mirror, I lingered examining my reflection. I held the dress against my body and ran my hands over the soft satin material. Was I confident enough to wear this dress? I blushed deeply at the thought of heating things up just a little bit more as I slipped the halter dress over my head. The fabric cupped my breast like a familiar lover only to drift lazily down to my knees. I stifled a giggle with my hand. Feeling almost shamed, I wondered how much was too much for an angel to handle. I was determined to find out before the night was over.

I stood in front of the mirror and stuck one velvet-soft leg out for inspection. The black, high-heeled sandals I'd chosen perfectly set off not only the dress but my legs as well. I could hear faint sounds of movement out in the living room and knew Elvis must have finished getting ready. I took one final look at myself in the mirror before I rejoined my date for the evening.

When I entered the living room, Elvis was seated on the couch with that crossed leg of his jiggling away again. It seemed to be more of an involuntary movement then one out of nervousness. However, I couldn't help but notice it went still when I stopped in the doorway. Slowly he stood up, and his approving gaze moved up and down my dress. I smiled when I saw that we'd both dressed in black.

"Whew, Lordy!" He walked around the table and reached for my hand. He spun me carefully around to get a better look and flashed that famous grin.

"You're very handsome yourself," I said.

"You like?" He took two steps back for me to get a better look.

"Yes sir, I sure do."

He was stunning in a black long-sleeved shirt. His shoulders were wide, though his chest was not overly stout. I liked to think the top three buttons were open for my visual pleasure. Oh, he knew what he was doing all right. He'd had years to perfect the look, and it truly left nothing to improve upon.

"We bought you those pants?" I asked as I noticed his black pants fit him a little more snugly than I'd remembered.

"Well, yes and no. I adjusted them a bit."

I didn't know how he managed that, but I didn't care. All I knew was he looked fabulous. But he might have looked too good. I suddenly became concerned that he might draw too much attention. A good-looking man like this gets more then just a few glances. I was nervous someone might be the wiser.

"Not good?" He asked with a hint of insecurity.

"No, no." I assured him. "It's very nice."

"What's wrong, Sam?" He said with a bit of frustration. He wasn't used to a woman's scrutiny.

"Well, you look so much like yourself. I'm just worried we'll have a problem." He watched me circle around him, my brows knit in concentration.

"Well, I can't change my face," he laughed and turned with me as I circled him again.

"No, you can't, can you?" I said absently while I pictured him in a mustache and beard. I finally had a man whose company I adored and was proud to be with, but whom I could never parade in public.

"Sam," he said sternly.

I looked up to frowning disapproval and smiled innocently.

"I'm not changing anything. It's a night club, it'll be dark," he stated defiantly.

"Well, then you'll just have to be an Elvis impersonator," I said with a deep sigh as I got my coat.

"What?!"

"I mean, an Elvis tribute artist." I recanted. "I forget they like to be called that now."

"I don't see the point of . . ."

"Everybody will believe it. After all, you're a dead ringer!" I said laughingly as I headed for the door. "Shall we go?"

The club was just down the street from my residence. Elvis didn't utter a word during those few miles. I could tell by his silence he was nervous with the roll he was going to play. Even so long after leaving this Earth, it seemed his fame was still a force to be reckoned with. I pulled into the bar's lot and tried to ease his worries as we parked.

"We might not have to deal with anything tonight. I just wanted a plan, just in case." I took his hand to get his attention.

"I know. Let's find a dark, private table and hope for the best," he said as he got out. He walked to my side to open the car door for me.

Daltons was my favorite pub to drop into for great music and food. I tried to see it through Elvis' eyes as we walked toward the front door. Although housed in an old brick building that rightfully gave it the look of a well-established, family-run business during the day, this night it was dressed up with a brightly lit marquee and blue twinkle lights that outlined the flat roof.

Elvis smiled and held open the big solid oak door for me to enter. I took a deep breath to calm the sudden flutter in my stomach. From the quiet of the parking lot, the cacophony of people, plates, and music was almost unnerving. At our right was a long line of regulars bellied up to the bar. The black, solid oak bar top was so long that it extended the entire length of the establishment's east wall. Seemingly more monstrous were the iron-framed mirrors just behind it that reached to the ceiling. After I'd taken a quick glance around, I immediately saw where we needed to go. I made a bee-line for a table near the dance floor, and looked back to see if Elvis was keeping up. He smiled again as we headed for the darkest part of the room to a table that was just enough off the dance floor to be barely lit.

"Well, this is dark. I hope I can see what I'm eatin'," Elvis said as he pulled my chair out for me to take a seat.

"If you miss anything, I'll be sure to tell you."

He smirked as he took a seat next to me and scooted his chair closer to mine. I handed him a menu and opened one for myself, even though I had the entire four pages memorized. I glanced over the top to see the familiar figure of my usual waitress making her way through the tables and bodies toward us.

"Hello, young'un'!" Tammy, my favorite waitress, exclaimed. Elvis stood as she hugged me hello. "Sam, darlin', who's this fine gentlemen your with tonight?"

She reached out through the smoky air and shook Elvis' hand, and he graciously accepted it into his two. Everybody was a fine gentleman to Tammy. She was a sweet-natured person who thought the best of everyone, sometimes even after being proven otherwise.

"This is Jon," I said, looking at Elvis. "Jon, meet Tammy."

"Nice to meet you ma'am," Elvis said politely.

"Oh, honey, he's polite and handsome? Keep this one, sweetie," Tammy said as she flung a lock of her long blonde wig over her shoulder. She officiously flicked the end of her stubby pencil with her tongue and looked at us expectantly.

Daltons was known for their Southern-style, home-cooked food. Staples included meat and potatoes—the wise would not ask for anything that involved tofu. All the food was made by Mother Dalton, and she cooked for her guests the way she had been taught to cook by her mother and her grandmother before her: lots of grease, batter, and gravy came with every dish she made. My favorite was her fried chicken, and Elvis took his chances with the meatloaf.

We sat in a moment of silence after ordering and watched the rustling about the room. As people talked in a low rumble and laughed uproariously, any private conversation was virtually impossible. The jukebox suddenly turned on, and music flowed out into the room. I chuckled, reminded of the saying that music calms the savage beast as the patrons' commotion settled down a few decibels.

"Do you come here a lot, Sam?" Elvis' voice broke into my thoughts.

"You don't know?" I said mischievously into eyes that narrowed in playful teasing.

"I'm a busy man, sweetheart. I'm not there watching every little move you make."

"Well, that's a good thing to know." I blushed from thoughts I needed to keep to myself.

"'Course, there was that one time . . ." He said with eyes that danced in laughter.

"What?" I coughed water out from my windpipes.

"What was his name now?" He placed an index finger on his lips and looked up at the ceiling. "Bobby, I think it was."

My mind was stuck on pause as my mouth hung open in shock.

"Bobby?" I questioned, not believing what I was hearing.

"Hmmm, handsome young man," Elvis said while looking at me over the rim the water glass from which he sipped.

"We were twelve!" I said in amazement that he even knew this story.

"Yup, that boy was a keeper!" He chuckled and set his drinking glass down.

"He picked his nose!"

"You're not going to hold that against 'ol Bobby boy, now are ya?" His laugh threatened to turn into hysterics as he became tickled by his own wit.

I leaned back into my chair and crossed my arms defensively across my chest. I watched him try to catch his breath. Off in the distance, I could see Tammy coming back with our meal.

"Shhh, here comes our food," I said and pointed her direction.

"Al-a-woochy." Elvis threw his hands into the air in praise, as though he was in church. "Saved by the food."

Still laughing, he leaned over and planted a firm kiss on the side of my cheek. I smiled slightly at his child-like behavior and watched him unfold his napkin onto his lap.

"Here you go, love birds. Enjoy, now." Tammy said as she placed our plates in front of us.

"Thank you ma'am." Elvis said and smiled gratefully at Tammy.

We sat in accepted silence and enjoyed our meal. My mind would not rest as I watched the bar become more crowded. I turned to Elvis and could see nothing but ease on his face as he finished his meal. I tried to release my own tension, hoping he'd know best if there was trouble brewing.

"That was some meal." Elvis said as he put his fork down and stretched back against his chair.

"It's always good here."

"You have a healthy appetite for such a little girl," he said and looked at my cleaned plate.

"I can eat more then that," I admitted. "I was holding back."

"You've gotta be kidding."

"Nope. I have to be careful not to eat everything they put in front of me."

"Well, I don't know if I want to see that. You have such a pretty little frame, you'll get fat!" He joked and poked my side with his index finger. I squealed like a little schoolgirl until I heard my name being hollered from across the restaurant.

Worried at first, I looked up quickly. I relaxed when I saw the source. My good friend Jimmy was weaving his way through the maze of people, waving excitedly. His band was the reason I'd wanted to bring Elvis tonight. Jimmy was a phenomenal musician and had been since we first met in high school. We had tried to date for a while, but my father quickly put an end to that when he learned Jimmy had formed a band. I still prickled with anger when I remembered my daddy, dressed in full minister regalia, paying a visit to Jimmy's parents to discuss the two of us dating. By the time he left their home, Jimmy's parents feared for our very souls. Poor Jimmy didn't have an easy time honing his music after that until he moved out of their home. Regardless, we'd remained fast friends through school to the present.

I stood up as he got to our table, and we hugged and greeted each other enthusiastically. Jimmy hadn't grown up to be a tall man, but his unkempt blonde hair and green eyes gave him a beach-boy look that no woman could resist. He was just as boyish and charming now as he was in high school.

"Sammy girl, where have you been?"

"Oh, working too much, you know." I started to turn to introduce Elvis, but he had already stood up beside me and was extending his hand.

"I'm Jon. Nice to meet you," Elvis said politely and firmly shook Jimmy's hand.

"Oh, hey. Nice to meet you. I'm Jim." Jimmy's eyes narrowed slightly as he leaned forward to get a better look at Elvis.

"Uh, we just met," I said to draw Jimmy's attention back my way. He had known me for a long time and was not easily fooled, which made me very nervous.

"Hmm, that's right, we did." Elvis nodded in agreement and grinned at Jimmy.

Both men held each other's gaze for a tense moment. I assumed Elvis found the standoff humorous, as he smirked through the entire encounter. He looked Jimmy in the eye and never wavered. Poor Jimmy tried at first to pretend the stare didn't bother him, but in the end he just averted his eyes back to me and shook his head.

"Well, I better get started here, Sammy, before we get fired or something. You guys staying for the music?" Jimmy had turned back to Elvis, but asked the question of me.

"Yes, we're going to stay awhile, I think," I said for the both of us.

"Alrighty, then," Jimmy said finally looking at me. "We'll talk later, Sam. You guys enjoy the show."

Before Jimmy turned to leave, he winked in my direction. I quickly looked behind me and was relieved to see Elvis had taken his seat. Thankfully, Elvis hadn't seen Jimmy curl his lip up in an exaggerated impersonation and laugh silently as he left. Elvis sat adjusting his shirt cuffs, unaware of Jimmy and I sparring. I looked back at Jimmy as I sat down and was horrified to see him still in character, twitching his legs as he walked back toward the stage. Good grief, he must be thinking that I'd finally gone overboard and was dating a tribute artist. Until, and if, I could ever straighten that idea out, I'd just have to let him think I was trying to live out a fantasy.

"Jimmy and I went to school together. We've known each other for almost ten years now," I explained. It was odd that I felt compelled to explain, as though I'd been caught red-handed.

"Yep, I could see he was quite comfortable around you," said Elvis as he put his arm around the back of my chair.

"His band is really a group of talented guys," I said. I still felt like I had to mend fences.

Elvis only sipped his soda and smiled knowingly over his glass at me.

The tables around the dance floor were beginning to fill up with people who had come to hear Jimmy and his band. The dinner crowd had gone, and the music crowd had taken its place. Jimmy and his band-mates bounced out of the wings onto the stage and were greeted with a warm rush of applause. The locals were familiar with this band's music, and most came ready to dance. They gathered in a tight, crowded bunch in front of the stage and out onto the dance floor. Others who came just to listen populated the tables on the perimeter, mostly couples concealed in low light for ultimate privacy.

Jimmy kicked off the evening with an old B.B. King number. Elvis smiled as the crowd hollered its approval. We watched as couples fanned out onto the darkened and cozy dance floor. Jimmy had B.B.'s style down, and for a moment stopped the crowd's collective motion with his passionate guitar solo. I stood to whistle my support for Jimmy over the crowd, but stopped as I saw Elvis' eyes widen. A busty blonde passed our table, her low-cut, sleeveless blouse clinging closely to what little skin it covered. A man followed helplessly behind her, oblivious to all except what moved as she walked.

"Have mercy," said Elvis, his eyebrows upraised. "Where's that woman's clothes at?"

We watched as the couple interlocked legs and began to sway to the music. The women melded with her dance partner, who clearly enjoyed himself every step of the way.

"Well, he doesn't seem to mind." I offered up.

"It never ceases to amaze me, baby." Elvis said, as he sat back in his chair and laughed.

Elvis watched the near-pornographic show on the dance floor. His reaction entertained me more than Jimmy's band. When Elvis saw that I was enjoying his shock, he stopped carrying on about the under-dressed woman.

"Oh, come on," he said and grabbed me by the hand. I willingly followed him out onto the dance floor. I hadn't worn this night-on-the-town dress for nothing!

As any loyal fan would, I knew that Elvis was not one to dance much, so I had not expected this gesture. He held my hand and led me out onto the floor. I watched couples move into each other's arms and longed for Elvis' arms around me, but he had other ideas. He released my hand and moved out on his own. I could see his smile as he turned to face me. His shoulders moved to the rhythm, and he slid one of his long legs out in front of him. In a casual leaning stance, he watched me approach. The singer's voice and the slow beat enveloped the floor in a sensual rhythm. My heart melted as Elvis nibbled his lower lip while he got into the music's funky beat. I was reserved at first and took my spot all too far away from his arms. As the music played on, I became more relaxed and soon was able to meet his gaze with some confidence.

I blushed at subtle movements his body made as he moved to the music. In perfect timing, he rolled a shoulder in my direction. Laughingly, I shook my bare shoulder back at him. I was not an accomplished dancer, but I did enjoy the freedom of moving to music. I noticed people watching us and wondered if they could feel the electricity between us.

I had finally let go and was getting caught up in the music when I noticed a smooth sensual hip gyration from my dance partner. I laughed in embarrassment and glanced around at the people flanking us. He only smiled and continued to watch me dance. When I couldn't bring myself to copy his movement, he did it again. I tried to contain my laughter and instead mustered up all the femininity I could. I swayed my hip forward in what I hoped was an irresistibly sexy move. Elvis laughed and sprung forward. He grabbed me to him and kissed my neck as we hugged. I was finally in his arms and happy to be guided by his perfect rhythm. He had no fancy dance steps, but rather just held me close and slowly swayed from side to side. I closed my eyes and completely gave myself up to the moment. I was moved by swaying hips commanding me to follow his led.

When the music stopped, I felt it only when he released me, as it was playing on in my head and heart. Everyone on the dance floor clapped. I turned toward the stage and also clapped, hands over my head, for my dear friend. Before I could lower my arms, black sleeves slipped around my waist from behind and held me firmly. I continued to clap amid the crowd as it whistled and screamed for more.

"Thank you, thank you everyone." Jimmy squinted into the stage lights and shaded his eyes. "We have a very special guest in the house tonight."

Even in the thick of the bouncing crowd, Jimmy's eyes met mine and twinkled with mischief. How my heart stopped beating and pounded in my ears at the same time, I'll never figure out. There was no place to hide and no time to squeeze through all the bodies to escape. I could only brace myself for the worst.

"Ladies and gentlemen . . ." Jimmy began as the horn section gathered behind him.

"Mr. Elvis Presley!"

Jimmy pointed out to the dance floor in our direction, and the crowd parted around us. Elvis abruptly stopped nuzzling my ear and tensed from head to toe as his name hung in the air. Slowly, he lifted his head and looked up at the stage. All eyes were focused on us.

"I'll be a son of a . . ."

Elvis left his curse unfinished. I turned to see a look of anger on his face. His eyes flashed fire and the muscles in his jaw flexed rapidly. The first few bars of "2001: Space Odyssey" sounded with great effort from the three-person horn section on stage. Elvis dropped his arms from my waist and fidgeted uncertainly. Everyone waited for his response.

"Come on, Jon, do it for Sam!" Jimmy yelled from the stage. "Ladies and gentlemen, I hear Jon is an Elvis impressionist. If we clap real loud, maybe he'll come up here and sing a song for us."

I turned to Elvis as the last few bars of the famous number grew stronger.

"You don't have to do this." I had to yell into his ear over the roar from the encouraging crowd.

Elvis glared over the top of my head at Jimmy. The band slid into the intro bars of C.C Rider, and Elvis disappeared from my side. He headed for the stage with long, effortless strides. The crowd on the floor both parted to let him through and followed behind him in one mass. The gap closed up and left me in its wake. I stretched up on my toes to see. Suddenly, he appeared on the stage and stood face to face with Jimmy. Elvis' smile doubled as a snarl, and he looked down hard at Jimmy, just inches apart. Jimmy took a wise step back. Elvis looked out at the crowd, and his face finally softened as he brushed past Jimmy and stepped up to the microphone. The crowd gasped as the stage lights hit his face. A woman's scream rose from somewhere far in the back of the bar. Elvis squinted and leaned forward, but the crowd was too thick and the lights too bright for him to pinpoint which female was already calling out for him.

"Behave yourself, now," he said into the microphone, his voice deep with that all-too familiar drawl. He stood confidently and let the crowd's receptive enthusiasm wash over him.

The screams only got louder as his voice echoed through the bar. The crowd was caught up in the moment. I moved more to the side of the stage but still struggled to get out of the crowd's way. The mob pushed toward the stage in a collective mass. When the introduction to C.C Rider came around again, Elvis didn't miss it. He jumped right in and claimed the microphone like a tiger does its prey. He snatched it up and brought it to his curled lips while his left leg shook with the scandalous tremors that had brought him world-wide fame.

"Oh, C, C, C Rider. Oh, see what you have done . . ." Elvis turned and nodded in Jimmy's direction.

"Ya, ya, ya." Jimmy grudgingly chimed in as backup.

"I said C, C, C Rider. Oh, see what you have done."

Elvis looked down at the front row, now full of girls. He broke out that million-dollar lopsided smile and was instantly rewarded with screams for more. I could not believe my eyes and barely could feel my legs. I involuntarily clutched my hands over my heart—I was captivated and watched every move he made. From the way he exaggeratingly rolled his eyes and provoked yet another stream of squeals from the women to the odd way the little finger on his right hand curled from an old football injury that never healed correctly, I caught it all. My inspecting eyes missed nothing.

"Girl, you made me love you, and now, now, now, your lovin' man is gone."

Elvis gripped the microphone with his right hand and closed his eyes, seemingly nodding his agreement with the lyrics of the song.

"C, C, Rider." Jimmy echoed while keeping his eyes on his guitar.

"Well I'm goin' away, baby. And I won't be back 'til fall."

Elvis smirked at Jimmy as he unbuttoned the cuffs of his shirt and rolled them up a notch. I looked around to evaluate the crowd, but only I seemed too aware of the sparring between Elvis and Jimmy. The rest of the band was oblivious to the exchange and were absorbed in returning the energy of both the men and women who had surged to the stage.

"If I find me a good girl, well I won't, won't, won't be back at all . . ." Elvis extended one long finger in Jimmy's direction as he finished the line. "Let see what you got, son."

At first surprised, Jimmy quickly recovered and stepped to the front of the stage to take the guitar solo. As Jimmy played, his left hand flew up and down the guitar neck and his right expertly finessed each string. Elvis watched and smiled as he rested his hands upon his hips. Girls screamed and men howled their approval for both performers.

"Ya, I'm going. Going away, baby, and I won't be back 'til fall . . ."

Elvis pointed to the statuesque blonde we'd seen earlier who pushed up to the stage for a better look. She squealed in delight.

"If I find me a good girl," Elvis shook his head at her and never stopped smiling. "I won't, won't, won't, be back at all."

I laughed as Elvis expertly played to his female spectators. He turned his back to the audience and threw out his hand, motioning to the band. The experienced musicians quickly fell into a slow, funky beat.

"I said, C, ahh . . ." Elvis growled into the microphone and looked back at the drummer. "I said, C!"

I jumped in my skin as the drummer suddenly came to life. He slammed out a heated drum riff as Elvis growled into the microphone and urged him to take it on home. The drummer made a final slam on the symbols and the bar erupted into a deafening roar. Elvis again faced the crowd, and a humble smile beamed across his face.

"Thank you," he said as if truly playing a concert. "Thank you very much."

He squinted to see out into his audience. I waved wildly, hoping he was looking for me. His eyes lit up when he finally spotted me stage side and winked in my direction. My eyes moisten and my throat tightens whenever I think about that night. I will always remember it as the time I finally got to see Elvis Presley live on stage.

"Give it up for Jon, ladies and gentlemen!" Jimmy yelled into the crowd.

Elvis wiped a bead of sweat from his cheek and smile modestly. The crowd roared and Elvis nodded his humble thanks back. Before he left the stage, Jimmy leaned over and yelled into his ear. I tried to read Jimmy's lips from a distance as Elvis smiled and shook his head no. Jimmy shook Elvis' hand as he left the stage. Before he could hit the bottom stair step, Elvis was mobbed by screaming women. I watched as they showed their appreciation. They stroked his arms and pulled at his shirt. A few of the women got in a shoving match over who would stay the closest to him. All the while, he was cool and collected, smiling and appreciating the attention.

"You were so good," one purred provocatively.

"Thank you, sweetheart," he said kindly and he tried to inch his way out of the crowd.

"Oh, you look so much like him!" The busty blonde gushed as she grabbed his arm.

"Thank you," said Elvis as he removed himself from her grip. "Excuse me."

"You should die your hair black!" I heard one woman yell as he walked my way.

Elvis looked like a man on top of the world. He walked with a spring in his step and a broad smile across his face. As he got closer, I could see small beads of sweat on his forehead. He swooped me up off my feet, spun me around, and slid me over his heated body. He was damp and moist as though he'd just stepped away from a karate workout. I hugged him anyway, happy to share in his excitement.

"You were fabulous!" I said in his ear.

He pulled me back to look at my face and kissed the tip of my nose.

"Time to go, baby girl."

Elvis grabbed me by the hand and led the way out. He practically drug me as I struggled to keep up with his long strides. What seemed like every person in that bar tried to catch him to pat him on the back, shake his hand, or plant a kiss on him as we tried to work our way out. Every set of eyes were on us. Once finally outside, we jumped into my car like robbers leaving the scene of a crime. I waited until we were well out of the parking lot to drop the convertible down and let the wind whip through our hair. Elvis let out a loud holler.

"Woo!" He threw his hands up in the air and laughed that uproarious laughter that he seemed to do at anything even remotely funny. "That was unbelievable!"

"Yes, it was. I was getting worried for a minute, though."

"You were? Why's that?"

"Because those women were about to lose their minds," I said, stunned that he had to ask.

"Ah, yes. Especially that blonde who needed to get some clothes on. She . . . now she was the one I was worried about."

"Was she dangerous?" I said suspiciously.

"Oh, man. A boy could get in a lot of trouble with a woman like her." He smiled at me and examined my face as I drove.

"Well, it's a good thing you're not a boy."

"Hmm, good thing. Very good thing." He laughed lightly and wiped the last drop of sweat off the bridge of his nose.

I looked at him, and I knew what he was up to—I could tell by the way he watched me with those laughing eyes. Every comment he made had some underlying meaning, as if he was trying to get a jealous rise out of me.

"You're *trying* to make me jealous, aren't you?"

The examiner in me took over and I stared at him while waiting for his answer. He just sat there and looked so pleased with himself, I couldn't stand it. I was so distracted that I didn't realize the car was drifting into the oncoming lane.

"Watch it!"

Elvis quickly pointed to the road ahead, but what caught my attention was the look on his face. I turned back in time to see two headlights coming fast right for us—or was it us coming right for them? *I'm going to die next to Elvis,* I thought in the nanosecond before my reflexes took over. I wrenched the wheel to the right and then back to the left to keep from oversteering us right into the ditch.

"Sorry," I snickered.

"You're going to get us killed," he said excitedly.

"Boy, you'd really get fired then." I laughed. "Nobody dies twice!"

Nobody made me laugh over nothing at all like my mother, and since her death I had forgotten what a good case of the giggles felt like. After nearly killing us both, Elvis and I looked at each other and just fell into eye-watering, stomach-aching fits of laughter.

"Whew, man" he said while he tried to catch his breath.

He was so much fun to be around. As I watched him try to regain his composure, it dawned on me: I'd always imagined him just as he was that night. He was light-hearted, humorous, and most importantly, a down-to-earth human being. *What will it be like when he's gone from my life,* I wondered as I took the last turn into my neighborhood.

Not until we were parked and getting out of my car did I start to feel the long day wear on my body. I opened the door to my house and stepped inside, glad to be home. In quick succession, I kicked off one and then the other sexy black sandal and padded barefoot to the kitchen for a glass of water. I was familiar enough with Elvis now that I no longer treated him like a guest who needed an invitation to sit and be comfortable. He sat right down and kicked his feet up onto my coffee table. I returned with a glass of water in hand and caught his propped up feet still shaking to a drum beat only he could still hear.

"I'm exhausted," I admitted.

"Mmmm."

He sat with his arms crossed and eyes half closed, probably going over his performance one more time. The silence was a drastic change from our hysterics just moments ago in the car. I looked down at the glass of water in my hand. The wall clock took on an Alice-in-Wonderland feel as each second passed with a pronounced tick. After the pace and emotional turmoil of the last few days, I found the silence to be far from peaceful. It actually began to make me edgy.

"I think I should say good night now," I said, if nothing else to get him to look at me instead of through me.

"Yes," he said as he shook his head slightly and got up to approach me. "I think that would be a good idea."

He reached for my hand and casually brought me to him. I closed my eyes in anticipation, and was rewarded his sweet, soft lips upon mine. The kiss ended too quickly. I opened my eyes and stared into a swirling pool of mysterious eyes.

"Now would be a good time," he said.

"Hmm? For what?" I was lost in the moment and laid my head upon his chest.

"... for you to go to bed."

"You said that already." I reminded him, as I fiddled with the top closed button on his silky black shirt.

"Alone," he said and placed his hand over mind.

"Oh." I stepped away from him.

"Now, Samantha," he said with that smirk and his hands on his hips as he waited for me to do as he asked.

"Okay, okay," I said like a disappointed child.

I turned away and shuffled down the hallway. I could feel him watching me as I approached my bedroom. I wondered if a battle was going on inside of him between the man and the angel.

"Elvis, won't you come tuck me in?" I spun back around just before I entered my bedroom.

"Get to bed, baby girl, before I have to come and paddle your behind," he called back sweetly and pointed at the doorway behind me.

"Oh, really?"

"Shhh ..." He waved me off while shaking his head at my antics.

"Alright ..." I sighed and opened my door. "Oh, I almost forgot."

I turned toward him again and this time he squinted at me in reprimand. It was as though I was eight years old again, pulling out all of my stalling tactics to avoid ending the day.

"I was only going to ask what it was Jimmy said to you tonight, at the end of your song?"

"He asked if I was going to hurt you," Elvis said as he relaxed his stern stance.

"I see." I said and again opened my bedroom door. "Good night."

My angel said good night one last time as I shut myself into my sanctuary for the remainder of the evening. As I undressed, I thought about the look Elvis had on his face when Jimmy asked him that question. In slow motion, I replayed seeing Elvis as he shook his head no. I searched my heart, and I knew the true answer.

# CHAPTER 5

It had been a long time since I'd awoke to the Lord's music on a Sunday morning. In the house where I grew up, Sundays started early. Daddy would be rehearsing his sermon for the day in the bathroom mirror as he shaved. My mother would be cooking breakfast happily, her apron laid over her Sunday best. The smell of biscuits floated around on waves of church music that played throughout the house.

This was my first Sunday with my guest. I was awakened by a familiar gospel song. The words to "I John/Amen" came flooding down my hall.

"Amen. Amen, everybody sing..."

Elvis' beautiful voice fast approached my bedroom door as I yawned. I rolled over just as my door flew open, and Elvis stood before me. He was dressed in a beautiful white suit, blue shirt, and white tie. I shrunk into my covers to hide my old pajamas and tried to straighten my hair with my hands.

"I say, amen. Hmmm..." He held the last note, arms out at his sides, obviously happy to be conducting his one-man choir. "Good morning, Sam. It's Sunday-go-to-meeting, and you're not ready yet?"

*Where did he get that suit for church?* Though it looked familiar, I was sure it hadn't been part of our shopping spree.

"God does provide," he said.

Yet again, he left me wondering if angels could indeed read minds. Truth was, he probably did. Sadly, I never asked.

"I don't go to church."

"Today you do, sweetheart," he said matter-of-factly.

"Today?" I repeated. "I don't have a church to go to today."

"Sure you do." I saw that spark in his eyes that always meant mischief.

It didn't take too much for me to guess of which church he spoke. I covered my head back up and hoped he'd go away. I closed my eyes and I huffed out a sigh of frustration. *Maybe if I lay here long enough he'll give up*, I thought. After a moment of not having the covers yanked off and hearing no movement, I peeked out. He was still patiently waiting.

"Ah, Sam, honey. God says today's your day to go back to church. Now you don't want to get me into trouble with my boss, do ya?" I bounced on the mattress under the force of his hand patting my hip.

I twisted my face into a frown as I considered what he was telling me. I was not going.

"If you don't go, I'll have to go back. Now you don't want ol' Elvis to leave yet, do ya?" He said coaxingly.

My heart ached at the thought. It did cross my mind that he was just playing me against my heart. However, the God I thought I knew would make him go home. I was sure of that.

I flung the covers off and climbed around him to get out of bed. He moved quickly to avoid being knocked over as I stormed off. He could talk anybody into anything, I thought in agitation. I stomped into the bedroom bath and slammed the door. His laughter followed me from the other side.

"What's so funny?" I yelled through the closed door and then turned on the shower so as not to hear his reply.

I bet God made him an angel just so he could come down here and charm people. All in the name of God, I mumbled. I caught sight of myself in the mirror, horrified that my hair was fuzzy and knotted on the side I'd slept the most.

"Y'all think you're so smart," I called out as I violently brushed my hair.

*All in Gods plan*, I thought. That adorable, contagious laugh that could change my mood was a plot by God himself. This whole mess was one big plan put in place by God. Before I knew it, I was having my first talk with God in a long while. I did all the talking.

"I know what you're doing." I said as I swung open the bathroom door to a surprised Elvis who still sat bedside. I must have looked frightful in my bunny slippers and ratty pajamas, swinging a hair brush for emphasis.

"What am I doing?"

"I'm not talking to you." I said as I passed by Elvis and headed for my closet.

"Okay." He said and crossed his leg. He rested his chin onto his closed fist as he watched my tantrum play out.

"Sending me the one thing I could not resist." I ranted at God from inside my closet.

I threw sandals and a dress out of my closet and onto the floor and just as quickly traded them for a skirt and boots. With items in hand, I marched right past Elvis again and slammed the bathroom door.

"Is this your way of apologizing?" I yelled as I pulled a shirt over my head.

"For what?" He asked.

"I'm not talking to you!" I hollered again in frustration as I stumbled on one foot while trying to step into my skirt.

"Oh, not me again," he laughed. "Sorry."

"Oh, wait, I remember now, you're God. You don't answer to anyone!" I yelled at The Almighty as I stepped back to the mirror.

I grabbed a tube of lipstick and smeared it onto my lips, so upset I completely forgot to even brush my teeth.

"Nope, I'm only the child," I said mockingly. I grabbed a tissue and wiped my lipstick right back off. I switched to autopilot to load up my toothbrush and continue my monologue.

"And . . . . ro-re-the-ma-steller!" I spit out the toothpaste. "I mean, you're a mama-stealer!"

I accused God as I attempted to put on my boots, hopping around with only one boot on. My tirade slowed only so I could answer a timid knock on the bathroom door.

"Sam, are you decent? Can I come in?"

I had already forgotten all about Elvis. My hands shook with rage that had been building up inside of me. I opened the bathroom door without looking at him and returned to the mirror. I leaned over the sink with locked arms and was vaguely surprised to see how white my knuckles were as I gripped the rim. After a moment, I looked up to face my reflection. I didn't like what I saw: a woman filled with an unforgiving heart, mad at a God with whom she couldn't even have a good fight. Through the tears in my eyes, I could see Elvis behind me. His beautiful face was compassionate as he lovingly put his hands onto my arms. I looked away from him and my own reflection. I couldn't look at myself anymore, I felt too ugly. As I began to weep, uncontrolled anguish seeped from my very pores. Elvis slipped his arms around my waist and pulled me close. His strong arms embraced me from behind. My cries shook my very body until my knees could barely keep me upright, and I leaned into him for more support. He gently laid his cheek against mine, and his breath was warm on my tear-soaked face.

"Shh, baby girl. Let it all out. I know it hurts, honey."

I faced Elvis and crawled into his arms. His embrace was sturdy, and I slowly began to catch my breath. He gently worked his fingers into my hair and held my head firmly against his chest.

"You catch your breath, now," he soothed.

I rested against him and drew comfort from the warmth of his body against my face. His heartbeat was steady and strong and radiated through his shirt like a life force. I listened to its natural rhythm and marveled at the idea of an angel's heartbeat.

"I'm sorry." I sniffed after I'd finally managed to collect myself.

"No, now, none of that," he demanded and lifted my head up so I could see into his eyes.

"You cry if you want to."

He held my head between his two hands. I closed my eyes and breathed in his scent, so fresh and intoxicating.

"I'm here."

Yes, he was, and I was so grateful. God had taken my mother but had sent me an angel. Nothing made sense as I pondered my circumstance. I felt his lips brush my nose.

"Cute little nose . . ." He whispered with a tender smile as he gazed into my eyes.

My heart melted as he reached up and stroked my cheek with the back of his hand. My heart beat with love for a man I knew I could not have. With tear-stained cheeks, I shyly watched his lips as he spoke.

"I'm here just for you."

When he kissed me, it was light and caring. Not heated and urgent as it had been yesterday at the lake. My head swam with emotion as I lay at rest on his chest again. Entangled in his arms and so completely safe, I wanted to stay there for an eternity.

"Baby girl, God wants you to go see him. Go with me?" Elvis' words echoed inside his chest and against my ear as he spoke. He pushed me away and held me at arm's length. I resisted the urge to push my way back to him.

At that moment, I would of gone anywhere with him.

\* \* \*

My mind wandered as we drove to the church of my childhood. What would my father do upon seeing me? What about Elvis? Who would I say he was? I hadn't been to the church since my mothers' funeral. How would the congregation that I grew up with receive me? During the course of the last two years, my father tried to guide me back. But he was too close to my problem and not able to help. Instead of feeling closer to my mother while in his presence, I only felt that much more aware of the gaping hole in my life and heart that was left without her. It was easier to not be available when he called. Shamefully, that's what I had done for so long now. Until this day, I had not seen my father in more than two months.

As I pulled into the church parking lot, I saw the building through long-suffering eyes. It looked so small, with newer buildings now all around it in the middle of this thriving city.

Atlanta being in the Bible belt, it probably supports more churches per mile than schools and malls combined. The churches tower the skyline with some of the most modern architecture of this generation. Standard seating capacity reached as high as thousands inside these temples.

The church I grew up in was not of grand stature. It was at least a hundred years old. The building's faded red bricks and cracked white trim thick with years of paint gave it the look of an old, wizened elder compared with newer buildings. To accommodate our growing community, additions had been built over time in accordance with budget and practical need and without regard for aesthetics or architectural consistency. An uneven stone path guided the patrons from the old building to the new, which was mostly for bible study classes. My father had been the pastor now for twenty-five years. Some members had been attending for more then forty. Most had been baptized, married, and eventually would be eulogized, all right at this church.

The older members considered my father to be a young buck, but like the rest of the congregation, showed him affectionate respect as their leader. I couldn't help but remember how this congregation had been there for him during my mother's passing. The men dropped by to take care of his yard and house, while the women brought steaming containers of homemade food. I'd heard that many a night he had been invited to eat at their homes so he didn't have to dine alone. This kind of love and support also had been offered to me. Sadly, I had disregarded their well-intentioned phone calls along with my father's.

I got out of the car and stood by Elvis. Without a word, I inhaled deeply and walked hand-in-hand with him up to the doors. Now the only thing between me and this world from which I'd been hiding were the large wooden doors. I hesitated before I entered. Just days ago, I never would have imagined the possibility of me returning.

"You ready?" Elvis smiled and lightly held my hand. He looked so handsome in his Sunday best.

I braced myself and nodded. Today I had with me a very special new friend, ironically sent from the heavenly force I'd been avoiding.

Two people who were unknown to me greeted us as we entered. I smiled upon seeing the fresh-cut white roses that were arranged on small reception tables in the foyer. *No doubt from Mrs. Baker's rose garden*, I thought. She had always filled the church with the sweet bundles in every corner with an available table.

The church was alive with the low buzz of conversation as members greeted each other and caught up on the week's events. People milled around in the dimly lit hallways before being called to assemble in the main sanctuary for the morning services. I clutched Elvis' hand tighter as we continued. The sanctuary was brightly lit, mostly from sunlight that cascaded from high windows near the post-and-beam ceilings. I felt exposed and vulnerable. It wasn't long before the wayward pastor's daughter and her shiny guest were the focus of the low buzz.

"Sam!" I nearly jumped out of my skin as my name echoed above the other voices.

Mrs. Madeline Rudabaker was a woman of high regard in the church. She led the women's group that organized retreat weekends and bible study classes, among many other activities. She became an extension of family when I was a child and often spent time with me when my parents needed to be away at meetings for church business. She always smelled like homemade apple pie, and I affectionately called her Maddy.

"Hello, Maddy." I reluctantly let go of Elvis' hand so I could be wrapped up into her ample bosoms for a heart-felt hug. My breath caught in my throat as I noticed Elvis wandering off without me.

"Does your father know you're here, Sam?"

"No, Maddy, he doesn't. But I'll get with him later," I replied half-heartedly as I craned to see Elvis through the throng. I spotted him already chatting amiably with church members.

"It's sure good to see you here, child. We surely missed you, and I know your father will be thrilled to see you," said Maddy as she watched me closely.

"Who's the handsome fellow you have with you today?" Maddy continued and laid an insistent hand on my arm to bring me back to our conversation.

"He's a good friend of mine, Maddy," I said shyly. We both watched Elvis move through the church with self-confidence and ease.

"Well, love, he sure looks like an angel to me." She giggled and poked at me with her impeccably gloved hands.

"Oh, he is that, for sure," I agreed with such sincerity that Maddy looked at me sideways.

"Serious is it? Has he met your father yet?"

"No, but I'm sure he will today."

"Well, if he's close with God, child, your father will love him."

"Maddy, he's so close it would scare you." I said, matter-of-factly. "In fact, he's the reason I'm here today."

"Well, halleluiah! The boy will get a big hug from me!" She exclaimed.

Elvis was busy enjoying conversation with just about every man and woman in our church as Maddy determinedly set out in his direction. She took him by surprise as she grabbed him to her large frame and picked him right up off his feet. Elvis appeared small pressed against Maddy's large, rotund figure. He laughed nervously as he disappeared inside her hug.

"Well, ma'am, do we know each other?"

I could hear his muffled question as I headed to his rescue.

"My name, son, is Madeline Rudabaker," she said as she set him down and formally stuck out her hand. "I've been looking out for this child since she was a small tike. Sam tells me you're the new man in her life, a Godly man at that, she says."

"I sure try my best, ma'am." Elvis said and straightened his attire after Maddy's affectionate attack.

"You know who he looks like, Sam?" Maddy turned to me as if she'd just discovered electricity. "That dead singer you were so in love with. Oh, what was that boy's name?"

"Elvis Presley," Elvis interjected and looked at me slyly.

The conversation had taken an unsettling turn. I held my breath and hoped at any second we'd be called in to begin services.

"Yes that's it! You're the spitting image of him, son." Maddy agreed enthusiastically and took another hard look at Elvis.

"Why thank you Ms. Rudabaker. Elvis was a lucky man to have someone like Samantha care about him so much."

I casually took a half-step forward and slipped my arm around Elvis' bicep, partially to offer him support from the overly familiar Maddy and partially for my own comfort. He reached up, rested his free hand over my own, and patted it lightly.

"Sam, darlin', you'd better hang onto this handsome young man," purred Madeline.

"I plan on keeping him around for as long as he'll stay," I said and tried to match my words with a smile.

However, I knew in my heart that fantasy would have to end eventually.

Elvis only winked in response. I glanced around and realized that everyone seemed to be melting by what they assumed were two lovebirds in their midst. I was spared from offering any further explanation when the church band struck up a tune that suggested we should all be seated. Reluctantly, I guided Elvis to my proper place down in the first row. For the pastor's daughter not to sit down front while her daddy preached would be considered disrespectful. I certainly did not want to cause any problems, so I headed toward my rightful place. As we were seated, I wondered if I should have gone back to say hello first to my daddy. How would my father react to the double surprise of not only seeing his daughter, but then also seeing a man who looked an awful lot like Elvis Presley sitting right next to her? I would soon find out.

My father was a tall, strong man. At more than 6'-3" tall, he was a tower of a man to be reckoned with. When he walked out to greet the congregation, I was reminded of the air of absolute authority he naturally displayed. He walked right past me, and our eyes met. In that small space of time, his eyes lit up with surprise and love. For a wonderful moment, I felt the remnants of only the best of times between us. That light was quickly shadowed as his eyes moved to the man who sat beside me. I fully expected his brows to fold together in that disapproving look I'd gotten so often while growing up. Instead, I was puzzled when a look of peace washed over his face—a look I'd seen only when my father was deep in prayer. As my father and Elvis smiled at each other, my heart warmed, but I was also deeply confused. Something happened between them in that flash of time. Whatever it was, my father accepted it and moved on to the pulpit. I could only sit in stunned disbelief.

Daddy had a special gift when it came to giving a sermon. He could always reach out and touch every member of the church on a personal level. He took on his roll as their pastor not as a man greater or more divine then anyone else, but rather as a servant of God challenged with all of life's hurdles. Just like the patrons who filled his church every week, he had failings, too. However, once at home, Daddy displayed his parental guidance with strong authority, and he was never wrong. Maybe it had been my rebellious attitude that bolstered his firm stance with me, but only in church had I seen the softer side of my father. As a child, this had angered me and only fueled more debates in our household. Looking back, I could easily see what a wayward force to be reckoned with I had been.

As was the customary start of all my father's service proceedings, everyone rose to sing. The church had an accomplished group of musicians who volunteered every Sunday. As the music started, I pointed the hymnal book out for Elvis. I was used to not remembering every song in the book, but didn't want him to feel awkward. Elvis picked up the worn blue book and handed it to me with a smile. I suppose it was silly to think an angel would not know all of God's songs. Even as a man on Earth, he had been well versed in just about every gospel song ever written.

The music paused, and the congregation took its cue to sing. Elvis sung with a strong and vibrant voice. I stood and silently listened as he sung the hymns I'd grown up with. Though the entire church was singing, I could only hear his beautiful voice, a voice sweeter than I'd ever heard on any one of his records. I was lost in the moment. As I concentrated on the sound of the very breath he took in between notes, my vision began to grow fuzzy around the edges. I closed my eyes to regroup. A familiar sound in the distant background caught my attention. The sound grew stronger, and I recognized it as the indefinable, rhythmic beeping that had been invading my dreams. Soon, the lovely music of the congregation was gone, replaced by this incessant, grating noise. My heart began to race, and I had to sit down. *Am I dying?* I flinched as I felt arms encircle me and a familiar voice call my name

"Sam . . . honey. Sam, open your eyes." Elvis said sweetly.

My lids felt like weights held them down as I willed them to open, just a little at a time. I blinked in short, rapid spasms and attempted to adjust my still foggy vision. As I struggled to see, it occurred to me what was missing—no music could be heard in the sanctuary, just that infernal beeping.

"Sam," a deep voice spoke into my ear.

My vision finally cleared enough for me to discern the voice. I found myself looking into the face of my father. With loving concern, he kissed my forehead and sat down next to me.

"Daddy, what's going on?" I croaked. My throat felt like I had swallowed sandpaper, and I was still dizzy.

"It's okay, baby girl, we're here for you," he said in a broken voice.

"Daddy, I want mama," I cried and rolled into my father's arms. He held me just the way he had when I was small and afraid of the dark.

"I know. She's here with us, honey," he assured me. "She has been watching out for us both."

A sweet scent of lavender wafted gently by in a subtle breeze, just as it had in Salem. I smiled tiredly through my tears at my mother's familiar smell. Exhausted, I rolled out of my father's arms. I wiped my eyes with the backs of my hands and tried to steady my shaking body. I reached out for my angel and was relieved to see he had not left my side. He took my hand, and his touch brought me great comfort.

"That noise is so loud. I think I'm going to be sick," I said to Elvis and put my hands to my ears.

"Just relax, honey," he said as he lovingly brushed the hair away from my face with one hand and took my hand with the other.

"Daddy . . ." I looked at my father and struggled to form words.

"I know who he is, Samantha. I can see," he reassured me, without hearing even one word.

"Daddy... I'm sorry I've been... a big disappointment to you," I managed to whisper.

"Shh, baby girl. Let's not talk now. You rest."

My father reached out to me, and I laid my head against his strong shoulders. Elvis gently let go of my hand and laid it over my daddy's arm.

"Don't go," I begged. I could feel my time with him was ending, and I was not ready to say goodbye.

"It's time, Sam," Elvis said and leaned over me to look into my face.

"No."

In the end, that single word expressed my every emotion. Elvis only smiled an adoring grin—the same one I'd seen now many times. I felt the soft touch of his hands as he caressed my face.

"Don't you worry. I'll always be around."

He leaned toward me, and I raised my head, anticipating his kiss. He stopped short in a teasing manner. His eyes flickered playfully as he gazed into mine. He quickly kissed my nose, then left my side and walked toward the pulpit. The church was in complete silence as he stepped up onto the raised platform and nodded to the band.

"Let us sing," he said to his waiting audience.

A blinding light flooded through the windows behind him. I squinted into its glow as it engulfed him on the spot where he stood. With eyes closed and his smiling face upturned to the heavens, he was poised to sing. Though he had no microphone, his voice carried clearly throughout the church.

> *"Shackled by a heavy burden,*
> *'Neath a load of guilt and shame.*
> *Lend the hand of Jesus, touched me."*

His voice was suddenly joined by many others that sang just as sweetly.

> *"He touched me,*
> *And now I am no longer the same."*

I watched him up on that pulpit and saw the joy in Elvis' eyes as he gazed back at me. His smile lit up his face and told me he was truly a fulfilled man. It dawned on me that he was finally getting to do what he was meant to do. He stood tall up at that pulpit, his audience captured, just as they'd always been in the past. He stepped down from the stage and walked back to my side, bringing the bright light with him. He offered me his hand, and I willingly took it and rose from my seat

*"Oh since I've met this blessed savior,*
*And since he cleansed and made me whole."*

As he sang, I marveled at the angelic light that engulfed us both. I felt warm, loving arms encircle me, yet nobody held me. Elvis' hand grew tight around mine as his voice sang on in praise.

*"Oh I never cease to praise him,*
*Oh, he touched me, he touched me."*

Elvis' voice grew stronger. He reached around to place one hand behind my head and another flat against my forehead. He laid his hands upon me and my legs suddenly became unsteady.

*"And oh what joy that floods my soul,*
*Something happened,*
*And now I know,*
*He touched me and made me whole."*

With those final words, the building shook. As I savored his last sung note, my legs began to fail me. I felt a new sensation and realized I was floating upward. I rose higher and higher into the engulfing light, my body immune to gravity. I rode on a gust of the softest wind that carried me away like maple leaves on a cold fall morning. *Was I going to heaven? No,* came a voice in answer, a voice I heard plainly inside my own thoughts and not from outside my weightless body. My eyes were shut, but that bright, bright light penetrated my eyelids. I let go of all grounded thoughts and floated in a dream-like state.

In one relieved exhalation, memories came flooding back to me. They filed through my mind, one-by-one, as I relived moments in time. The moment I was told my mother would not live. I felt my body shrink in grief as I remembered her body lying in state for her funeral. I refused to watch again, and I pushed away. I floated as light as a soul. Through the entire experience, the once-menacing beep continually hovered next to me. Though I'd found it menacing up to this point, for some reason I couldn't yet explain, I knew that it had purpose. I knew I had to reach out, and I was now not afraid to do so. The closer I came to the unknown, the more the weight of the world returned. Like a spinning ride at a small town carnival, I was held in place. I squeezed my eyes shut and felt my stomach turn. As the ride came to a jolting stop, I was thrown forward. I laid perfectly still, afraid to move. The heaviness of being Earth-bound returned to my body. No longer was I a floating soul as I began to feel every inch of the ground on which I'd landed. My head pounded, and my back ached as if I'd been lying in the same spot for years.

Though my eyes were closed, I felt the presence of a cold world that waited expectantly for me. The beeping sound that for so long had been out of my reach was now beside me. I thought how it was not as mysterious as it once had seemed.

I forced my eyes to open. They resisted mightily against the sterile light over me. This new glow was not comforting. Fear and confusion began to take over. My focus was blurry, but I could hear machines beeping all around me. I looked around at the bed and the dull, gray room I was in. The only thing that was familiar was that infernal beeping. Tears filled my eyes as the sharp smell of bleach replaced my mothers' lovely lavender fragrance. I strained to turn my head and saw a couch to the side of my bed. A snoring occupant was wrapped up anonymously in a faded blue blanket. The sleeping guest didn't hear me.

I was startled by the sudden turn of a doorknob. A woman in monochromatic green scrubs entered the room. Suddenly, I understood. I was lying in a hospital bed. *Why am I here?* I thought earnestly as I watched the woman who I guessed was my nurse march in with a task in mind. Her on-my-feet-all-day shoes squeaked with every other short step as she crossed the room. With not one glance my way, she took out a chart from the foot of my bed. I tried to speak to her from within the mask on my face, but only groggy wordless sound came out.

Her head whipped up, and she juggled the chart in her hands as though it was hot.

"Dear Lord! Ms. Bennett, you're awake!"

The forgotten chart clattered to the floor as she rushed to my side. The snoring from the couch stopped with an abrupt snort, and the person unraveled himself from the tattered blanket.

"Mr. Bennett, Mr. Bennett. She's awake!" The nurse screeched.

My eyes widened at the horrible sight. My father rose from the couch. He barely resembled the man I knew. A fully bearded, overly skinny, and obviously under-spirited person looked out from the shell of what once was my father. He stood up with great effort, hair matted and many days past needing a shave. He approached my bed with his ashen face awash in confusion. Tears welled up inside his bloodshot eyes as he leaned over the bedrails to look into my face. A trace of tobacco smell followed close behind him, and yet my father had not smoked in almost fifteen years.

"Daddy, have you been smoking?" My voice sounded small and hollow inside the oxygen mask. "You smell."

"I do? I guess I must, baby girl, I'm sorry," he said and began to simultaneously laugh and cry.

He collapsed to his knees and laid his head on the bed next to me. His wispy body heaved with his sobs.

"Daddy?" I struggled to talk with my new rough and raspy voice.

"Yes, darling." He sat up and brushed the hair back from my forehead.

"Where's Jon?"

"Jon who, honey?" He questioned with a look of concern.

"Elvis, Daddy." My father knew the truth, and I knew I no longer needed to pretend.

"Oh, he's right here, honey."

I tried to sit up a bit and watched my father as he crossed the room, but I didn't see Elvis anywhere. Daddy grabbed a black object and brought it to the little table next to my bed. It was my portable compact disc player.

"I've been playing him for you every day," Daddy smiled through his tears.

Within that first hour, I had a room full of doctors, relatives and friends. Although they all wanted to talk at once, I managed to understand that I was in a hospital in Atlanta. I asked if they knew why I passed out in church. They quit talking long enough to exchange puzzled looks, and then my daddy took over. He chose his words carefully.

"Sam, honey, you've been here for weeks. You and Heather were in an accident in Boston," he said while stroking my face.

I knew that somehow he'd gotten his facts mixed up, and I tried to tell him what really happened. He put his hand to my lips and shook his head.

"No, Sam, don't speak, you've been through a lot. Just save your energy."

All the while stroking my face with one crooked finger, he told me that Heather was injured, but not seriously. She was at home, but not back to work just yet. Daddy told me how he'd made her go home, as she'd been in my room almost as much as he had. Tears ran unchecked down his pale, unshaven face when he told me the doctors weren't able to say when I might wake up.

"They don't know you, Sam. I knew you'd be back, honey," he said with a quiver in his voice.

The "small" accident Heather and I had had in Boston wasn't as unimportant as I remembered it. As he sat alongside my bed, my father assured me that Heather came out okay. I was relieved to hear she had only suffered minor cuts and a few deep bruises. I, on the other hand, had hit my head and shattered the front windshield. I had been taken to the nearest Boston hospital where I had laid in a coma. After about a week, the swelling in my brain was reduced somewhat, and I had stabilized enough for my father to have me returned home to Atlanta. The doctors in Atlanta had not given up hope and had daily encouraged my father that once the swelling went down further, I would awaken.

"How long have I been *here*, Daddy?" I whispered.

"Ten days, Sam," he said and wiped away the tears that would not stop.

People slipped in and out of my room for the remainder of that day. Some I recognized, some not, but all beamed and wiped their eyes. I was told my father had slept, prayed, and eaten right there in my hospital room the entire ten days. Many visitors had come and gone during that time to offer him support and to try to relieve him, but he would not budge. It was so hard for me to believe what my father said. How could we have such different versions? My time had been full of love and excitement, and yes, some sorrow, but the healing kind. I no longer felt the anger toward my father that I had, and although I still missed my mother, the empty spot in my heart felt much less so. I knew nothing of the story my father told me. The days I spent with Elvis were real, and I clearly remembered simple things in detail, like how he smelled so masculine and clean. I could still hear him teasing me so playfully. Though the mind is a mysterious realm, this was surely different. I could not convince myself that it had all been a dream.

"Daddy, my memory is so clear. I have real memories of the days after the wreck. You're telling me this is where I've been. What am I to do with that?" I asked and hoped in vain that he had an explanation. To realize my memories were false broke my heart.

"Maybe this dream was God's way of protecting you from the physical pain you must have been suffering," he offered consolingly.

My father tried to find a religious meaning to my dream. I couldn't help but wonder if my physical pain could possibly have been worse then the heartache I felt after I awoke.

In the days that followed, doctors ran tests and therapists worked my body. Everyone was in high gear to get me ready for my discharge back out into the world. Though the human body is an amazingly tolerant machine, it can quickly become fragile. Two weeks of stagnation took a huge toll on my body. Muscles that hadn't been used were deteriorating, and it was several more weeks before I was back on my unsteady feet.

When the time to go home had finally arrived, the nursing staff bid me farewell and good luck. They affectionately called me their miracle patient of the year. Between sheer luck, or perhaps divine intervention, and my own hard work and determination, I was able to leave without any long-term physical ramifications. Other than my heart's yearning for something that was not real, I was physically well and given a clean bill of health.

The day my father arrived to drive me home, I was dressed and ready to go before he even made it to my room. I was happier just to be in real clothes and not a drafty hospital gown.

"Ready, baby girl?' He asked as he came into my room for the last time.

"Yes sir. I sure am," I said and slowly rose from the edge of my bed.

I wanted to walk out on my own, but hospital policy dictated a wheelchair ride to the curb. Daddy pushed me along and smiled gleefully to everyone we passed. A line of nursing staff followed us to the door and stood waving as I got into the car. As we drove away, I looked back one last time. I was ever so thankful to go home.

"Your aunt Betty called me today." Daddy tried to make small talk as we drove.

I looked out my window as we turned onto the freeway toward home. My father never drove over the speed limit, which for once suited me just fine. I did not have an appetite for high speed and didn't expect I would for some time to come. I leisurely watched as big office buildings and one-story houses all passed by equally as slow as we crawled along in the right-hand lane.

". . . she would like for you to drop by and see her," daddy resumed and turned to look at me. "When you're feeling better, give her a call."

"Okay," I sighed without turning from my window.

We passed the Atlanta mall. The shopper's cars lined up on the street as they struggled to find a place to park. I smiled and remembered the look on Elvis' face the day we walked him in to fix his attire.

"Sam, what's wrong?"

"I'm just remembering shopping at that mall," I said casually.

"Oh." My father never understood a woman's fascination with the mall. "I've got a new series starting with this Sunday's sermon. Want to come?"

"What is it called?"

"An unforgiving heart," he said as he searched my face.

I smiled at his never-ending attempt to cure his daughter, even on the very day she's released from the hospital. If my father was anything, he was persistent.

"This was just something I'd been working on. I had to put it aside when you had your accident." He stumbled over himself trying to explain.

We passed Daltons just before the turn into my neighborhood. I twisted my neck trying to look as we passed by. I chuckled as I saw it's dingy state of affairs.

*My memory of Daltons was so much more romantic,* I thought. This building sadly wore crumbling faded bricks and weathered windowpanes that were badly in need of another painting.

"You don't want to go?" My father's voice rattled me from my daydream.

"No, Dad, I'll go," I said and was rewarded with a broad grin.

"You will?"

"I will."

He reached over and squeezed my hand. I imagined my mother looking down upon us, smiling. We held hands for the last few miles home.

# CHAPTER 6

During the course of the next two months, I remained busy getting back into my life. My health was a real question for when I could return to my job. I had to prove I was fit enough to fly, so I complied with every medical test asked of me. Whatever was necessary for me to be released back into the skies, I did it happily. I was thankful when the day finally came that I could count on work to help occupy my time.

Before long, the seasons were changing and fall was coming on fast. The nights were cold, but the days remained warm. Mother Nature's inability to decide which season she desired to showcase had the trees in my neighborhood completely baffled. Some wore leaves of orange and red, while others still tried to bloom, never giving up efforts to bear fruit.

One evening upon arriving back home at the end of a long trip, I pulled into my driveway without my customary eagerness to go inside. I remained in my car and just contemplated nature's seasonal tug-of-war in the tress around me. I could see Mrs. Jefferson next door studying me from her living room window. She had become ever so observant of my every move since my accident. Whether it was out of concern or curiosity, I wasn't sure. She knew of my coma because my daddy had asked her to collect my mail while I was away. Since my return, I'd often caught her staring at me as I sat in the car, as I sometimes did. I figured she must have written me off as crazy many weeks ago. I'd kept to myself and when home, I rarely went outside anymore.

Truth was, there were few in my life with whom I could share the events of those dreamed moments with Elvis. I had especially only told my father a little about those weeks that felt like only a few days to me. Though he surely found it fascinating, he was not able to grasp the depth of what had happened. I was never good at explaining matters of the heart with Daddy. Love had always been my mother's specialty.

Finally bored with my tree watching, I reluctantly got out and proceeded up to the house. I opened my door and entered without acknowledging Mrs. Jefferson. It saddened me a little that I no longer felt the joy in the simple pleasure of coming home. My private sanctuary, once comforting and safe, now held false memories around every corner. I stood thumbing through my mail just inside the doorway and struggled to accept my new reality. The urge to run and see if he had been waiting was hard to overcome.

It seemed it was only with Heather that I could share all the profound details of my adventure. Only with her could I bare my heart and my feelings of true loss and heartache. I had awakened her on many a night with a late night phone call and crying on the other end. She was always kind enough to let herself be kept up listening to my heartache until I could fall asleep again. Before long, it became habit to call on a whim when the need arose. The desire overcame me often, and that evening was no different once I'd arrived home.

"Sam, you're just going to have to be grateful for what sounds like the best damn dream of your life. Shoot, I'd have you hit me over the head if I could spend a week with Brad Pitt."

Heather always made me smile, and I loved her for being my one friend I could share anything with. I counted myself lucky to say I had at least one.

"I know," I said, as I sat down on the living room sofa and enjoyed a hot cup of chai-spiced tea.

I stirred intently with one hand and held the phone with the other. The smell of chai usually made me feel relaxed, but it wasn't working it's magic. Childishly, I twitched my foot and sent one navy blue pump sailing down the hallway. I felt rather gratified as I watched it bang against the hall closet door.

"You don't sound convinced," Heather said.

"Well, I'm not really. But I don't see what choice I have." I said as I agitatedly flung the second shoe down the hallway. I frowned with disgust when didn't make it as far as its counterpart had.

"You know what you need? You need to get out of that house and get back into living outside of work."

"Yeah?" I asked cautiously and felt a plan brewing.

"How about I come over, first thing tomorrow morning? We'll spend the day shopping and hit a spa.

"Alright," I agreed. It sounded harmless enough.

I'll pick you up about ten in the morning, and I'll plan it all." Heather said and then promptly hung up in my ear.

I pondered how ironic it was to have this dial tone beeping in my ear. I was sure Heather had the day all set in her mind before she even called. She needed to try to cheer me up just about as badly I needed cheering. As it was, tomorrow was my day off, and I had no plans.

I hung up the phone and thought about how having an event planned would surely help me get through the night. But the house was unnervingly quite, and, as usual, I was ready for bed but too restless to sleep. Instead, I wandered from room to room, lost in pondering the wonder of an afterlife full of angels.

I stopped in the hallway to look at a wedding photo of my mother. She was dressed in a long but simple white gown and made such a beautiful bride. I stared at her picture as if maybe she held the solution to my predicament. Intently I waited for the answer, but finally had to admit that no advice would come forth. I moved on, continuing in my search for a distraction. Soon I found myself at the doorway to my office. I paused outside it and questioned if I had the courage to go in. With a deep breath to steady my nerves, I opened the door and entered. I hadn't been in this room since I came home from the hospital. My heart sunk, and the little flicker of hope he was there died. I knew then that I had to take Elvis' face down from those walls. For the first time in my life, he wouldn't be present in my house. My heart continued to ache with a memory that wasn't real, and the photos only reminded me of what I'd never have.

As much as it hurt to admit, Elvis and I didn't know each other. We hadn't spent time in each others lives. He had come into mine in the same way he did every ones else's—through his music. Elvis reached out to the world, and the world embraced him in a love affair that was cut too short. I was only one in a million who shared in that love. That reality was hard to accept, but it was necessary for my own heart's survival that I try.

As I stood in that room, I pushed out the memory of Elvis sitting at my desk. If I closed my eyes, I could see him intently reading the very magazine that still laid there. I picked it up and noticed the front cover: *Elvis Gives Hope to a Dying Child*. The accompanying article had been written ten years earlier. The corner of an inside page was folded over to mark the spot—something that was not my habit.

Slowly I took a seat with the magazine in my hands. I remembered Elvis' intent face as he'd read it. My hands shook as I opened it to the marked spot. The leading sentence spoke of hope given to a small child who was dying of leukemia. I was sure I'd never seen this article before. It went on to chronicle the story of little Angela, who on her deathbed reported being visited by the angel of her mother's friend. Angela's mother had grown up listening to Elvis and had once met him during her youth. She'd been as close to a life-long fan as one could be. She had shared stories with Angela and shown her photos taken from the one-time meeting. A fantasy of friendship began a story that her daughter believed to be true. Just before the little girl had passed on, Angela told her mother not to worry. She said Jesus would send their special friend to take her to heaven. She was not to be scared, Angela told her mother. Your friend will be with me.

I cried when I read of Angela's passing peacefully in her sleep. The next day, her mother shared the story with the local paper about how the spirit of Elvis Presley took her child home to Jesus in heaven.

My tears flowed as I laid the magazine flat on the desktop. I neither could remember where I had gotten this collectable, nor ever having read it. The only memory clear to me was the sight of Elvis reading it himself. Had I read this before and brought it into the dream with me? Nothing was clear anymore. I couldn't help but question every feeling or memory I'd had in the last few months. The effort in even trying to rationalize such events exhausted me beyond comprehension.

I closed my eyes and imagined God watching somewhere from the heavens. I prayed for some peace in my soul. I needed to believe that finding this story had been a sign. Maybe that was all I needed to do: believe I had read Angela's article prior to my accident, then carried it with me.

I laid my head down on the desk and thought how simple this reasoning sounded. I hoped I had finally found something I could accept as the truth. The sweet feeling of sleep began to drift over me. Just as I was about to give in to slumber, the sound of running water captured my attention. I sat straight up in my chair and listened breathlessly to the familiar sound. Fully aware I was awake and not dreaming,

I walked to the doorway. The door creaked on it's hinges as I opened it and leaned out to determine the source.

My adrenaline raced and I forced myself to walk towards the sound. Though I fantasized of my angel, I tried not to get my hopes up again. *This was probably just a sprung leak in the facet.* My breathing escalated, and the hairs on my arms stood on end. *Was he here?*

The shower was indeed running, and the steamy air was warm as I inhaled. One would have thought someone had been enjoying a nice long shower at the end of a hard day. I wasted no time and walked right up to the privacy door. Nobody was there. Water ran hot into an empty stall full of steam. I questioned my fragile sanity, caring less about how a mysterious shower could have started on its own. I opened the door to look inside.

As if the space might hold all the answers, I entered in, clothes and all. I turned my back to the water, and my nightgown clung to my body. The hot water rolled over my shoulders and down my front. I allowed it to cascade over my hair and wash away the tears I was shedding. I steadied myself against the wet shower walls and struggled to imagine his every detail as he had once stood there. I could still clearly see his slender body relaxed by the simple pleasure a shower can bring. My tears continued unchecked as every cell in my body shed this grief for a lost love. I watched the water pool around my feet. My tears mixed with the water and swirled down the shower drain. I was lost within myself. I never even heard his footsteps.

Suddenly, cold air rushed inside my warm sanctuary as the shower door opened. I caught and held my breath as my heart raced in expectation. The smell of a familiar cologne drifted into the shower. Even before I turned around, I knew whom I would find behind me. He stood relaxed with one arm held against the shower door and his other propped up out of view. His blue eyes were locked onto mine, and his intense expression kept me riveted to the very spot I stood.

He had first come to me in a dream, just as God created him, naked and natural. This time it seemed our Earthly meeting would be much more mutually intense. The Elvis who stood before me commanded great authority. He was dressed completely in black, and his boots were shined to an obsessive gloss. The once natural brown locks now glistened the jet-black for which he was famous. His second manifestation to me screamed of power and masculinity. This Greek-God look made him excitingly dangerous. His blue eyes smoldered as they released mine. His gaze shifted down, caressing my body. My wet nightgown clung to my breasts, and his eyes lingered there admiringly. I nervously covered my chest with my hands. A smile threatened around the corners of his mouth, and he seemed amused by my shyness. His eyes returned to mine in a look of pure mischief. He didn't speak as he stepped into my world. I instinctively took a step back, only to be stopped by the shower wall. A slow smirk crept across his face. He continued forward and paid no mind to the water that rushed over his fine clothes.

"Miss me?"

I squirmed and tried to regain some composure.

"Am I scaring you, Sam, honey?" He spoke with concern, but his eyes danced.

"Yes," I admitted quickly and brushed at the wet hair stuck to my face.

He stretched out an arm on either side of me and braced himself against the wall.

"I couldn't let you go on questioning, now could I?" He said as he took a slow step forward so that we were lightly touching. His eyes were like deep pools that I could, and did, get lost in.

"I'm real," he whispered within inches of my lips.

"I, I see that," I stuttered and tried to clear my foggy mind. His full wet lips mesmerized me as he spoke.

"I missed you."

"I'm confused," I confessed unnecessarily.

"Mm, yes." He shifted his weight onto his other leg and settled in. "Let me make things real clear for you, honey."

He leaned into me, and our lips finally touched. He had me pinned where he wanted me, and it was where I wanted to stay. His kiss was soft and tender. My mouth willingly opened to let all of him in. My soul soared as our tongues danced together like familiar partners. My heart beat even harder when he softly moaned, lost in his own excitement. He held my chin at the angle he wanted as he expertly and ever-so-slowly explored my mouth. The heat between us added to the thick steam from the shower. When he broke away, I licked at the tingling spot he'd left behind on my lips. He pulled me away from the wall and brought me into his arms. I threw my arms around him, no longer shy. I pressed into him and tried to get even closer.

"I was so worried you weren't real," I cried. "Everyone said it had only been a dream."

"I know, baby girl. You just let me take care of you now."

He shut the water off and ran his hands through his wet hair. The water glistened on his beautiful face. His cat-ate-the-canary grin told me we weren't staying there. He took my hand and stepped out of the shower to lead me toward the bedroom. He stopped us bedside and turned to face me. My anticipation soared, as I looked into his fervent gaze. Gently, he brushed away a strain of my dark hair and caressed my shoulder. As if he wanted to allow me the time to stop him, he slowly hooked a finger under the strap of my nightgown and slid it off my shoulder. Ever so lightly, he floated a fingertip across my bare skin. I covered his hand with mine and stopped him.

"You'll catch death of cold," he murmured playfully.

I let his hand go and allowed him to remove my other strap. My gown fell to the floor. I stood before him, vulnerable and naked. He caressed my shoulders with warm hands that felt like velvet on my damp skin. His eyes lovingly took in my whole body in a way that no longer left me feeling self-conscious. I felt admired and longed for.

"You're very beautiful, honey," he whispered and took a step toward me.

"You're gonna catch death of cold," I whispered back.

I began to unbutton his shirt. That famous lopsided grin slowly crept over his face as he watched me work the first button. Suddenly, he covered my two hands with one of his. I looked up at him questioningly.

"Ah, ah, not so fast," he said lightly.

He scooped me up into his arms with ease. As if we were one, we fell onto my bed and rested side by side. His wet clothes stuck to my bare skin as he crooked one leg across mine. He pressed hard into my thigh, and I could feel his desire. I reached down for him, but he stopped my hand and brought it to his lips.

"I need to run this show, darlin'," he said and teasingly kissed my palm.

My frustration mounted. He mimicked my look by jutting out his own lips. I pretended to be annoyed at his teasing and turned my face away from him.

"Ah, now," he said laughing, turning my face back to him. "Good things come to patient little girls."

He spoke in total control, and yet his eyes told a different story. A look of longing and crumbling self control showed on his face as he scanned my eyes. He easily read their fiery message. As he reclaimed my lips, I was no longer forbidden to touch him. My body yearned for his. He leaned in harder and responded to my desire.

In quick but determined movements, I again attempted to unbutton his shirt. He gave in and rolled onto his back. Those eyes watched my every movement. He seemed amused as my hands worked determinedly on small buttons, trying to free him as quickly as possible. My hands shook as they stumbled over the tiny obstacles. He interrupted with a chuckle and removed his shirt himself. I began to eagerly touch him even before he had his shirt fully removed and tossed aside. He was amazingly thin, but he had a masculine strength about him that I could not resist. I crawled on top of him and laid my petite frame over his. His face flashed in sudden bashfulness as I examined his half naked body under mine.

"You're so strong aren't you? So masculine..." I required no answer as I ran my hands down his sturdy chest, admiring the feel of soft hairs between my fingers.

My heart fluttered when I looked up and saw the hunger in his eyes. Without a word, he reached up and ran his hand into my hair. I softly stroked his bare arm, as he held the back of my head in his palm. He pulled me down to meet his waiting lips. His kiss was eager from the start as he crushed me to his chest.

Distracted by each other's touch we barely noticed or even cared when a low rumble echoed through the room. After a long pause, hail began to strike the roof. The intensity and escalation of our passion was matched by the growing storm outside.

As one, we rolled over onto our sides. I unbuckled the belt of his pants as he sampled the nape of my neck. My breath caught in my chest as he nibbled upon my ear lobe. Outside, lightening struck and was immediately followed by a resounding crash. Elvis suddenly became still. He was no longer inside the moment as he listened to the threatening rumbles of the storm. My passion was curtailed when lightening struck ground just outside my bedroom window. A piercing white light filled the room. I was literally shaken right out of my trance.

"Ah!" I squealed like a child over the furious crack. "What was that?"

"It's ok, I'm here," he assured me with a light kiss to my lips.

I watched Elvis re-buckle his pants belt as he got up and walked to the window. Rain as hard as I'd ever heard hammered down as the storm raged. He returned to my side without speaking, but I already knew the truth behind the storm.

"You're not supposed to be here, are you? Are you in some kind of trouble now?"

He didn't answer, but just reached for his shirt. I loved him, that was true, but I couldn't let something awful befall him because of me. He silently climbed back onto the bed. I searched his face for answers.

"God is a God of forgiveness honey, you know that," he said with a steadying sigh as he pulled me to him. I rested on his chest as he stroked my hair.

"What is going to happen?" I hoped he would tell me something that would make it all better.

"Nothing darlin'. Fathers sometimes need to remind their children of the rules, that's all." He lifted my chin up so he could look into my eyes. "Sometimes the rules get blurry where love is concerned."

*Was he trying to say he loved me?* He searched my face for some understanding and, finding none, instead kissed my forehead.

"Don't you worry your pretty little head about a thing, just lay here with me for awhile."

"Are you going somewhere?" His heart beat steady and true in my ear as I laid my head back down on him.

"I'll be right here," he assured me.

"But, will you be here when I wake up?"

"You just sleep, baby girl, and dream sweet dreams . . . of me," he replied while kissing my lips every so lightly.

He began to hum a tune. The rain beat endlessly at my rooftop as the thunder and lightening gradually subsided. I fell asleep to the sound of his voice humming deep inside his chest. It settled my restless heart.

The next morning, I awoke to knocking and my name being called just outside my bedroom door.

"Sam, you awake?"

Heather was never late. I rolled over and squinted at my alarm clock. Sure enough, 10:00 a.m. on the dot. I quickly tried to regroup my thoughts. *Elvis!* I turned to find the other side of my bed empty. Though the rumpled sheets and covers certainly looked like they'd been occupied, Elvis was gone again.

"Hold on!" I yelled and seriously thought about revoking the house key I'd given her.

I jumped out of my bed, grabbed a robe, and threw it on. I pushed my feet into my bunny slippers as I looked wildly around the room. He had left no signs of where he had gone.

Heather grew louder outside my door as she carried on about seeing some man leave my house, and why wasn't I coming out?

I flung my bedroom door open and rushed right past my friend. I raced down the hall and out my front door. The bright daylight stopped me in my tracks, and I had to take a moment to adjust. I blinked impatiently and shaded my eyes while I scanned left and right. Heather's footsteps pounded behind me as she followed in hot pursuit.

"Sam, what is going on?" She watched in confusion as I squinted and repeatedly looked up and down the sidewalk.

"Did you bring that man home last night, Sam?" She scolded.

"Yes." I blurted out, then took it back. "No. I mean, well, he stayed over but not like that."

"I see," Heather said skeptically.

"You saw him? How long ago did he leave?" I still hung onto some string of hope.

"We chatted for a few minutes. I was shocked to see him coming out of your house, but he sure was a cutie," she admitted.

I turned to give her a disapproving look. How could she strike up a conversation with an unknown man who just walked out of my house? I guess I should have been grateful that she didn't do something irrational like knee him in the groin and ask questions later, but she sure could have done better than be sociable with him.

"Gee, it means the world to me that you approve," I said sarcastically.

"Well he had a hat on, but from what I could tell, he seemed pretty hot. Although, he was a little familiar," she mused.

Heather chatted away to nobody in particular as she talked through the mystery. Only when she stopped to take a breath did she see my irritation.

"What?"

"Never mind!" I threw my hands up and stomped back into the house.

"It's not a big deal, Sam. You're a grown woman, and he sure was a grown man! I mean, what are you so worked up about, I'm sure he'll be back!" She called after me in apology.

We never made it to the spa that day. Instead, we stayed at my house talking. I tried to share the basic details of what happened the night before. I could barely tolerate that just as I had been grieving for Elvis for what I'd hoped was going to be the last time and was finally ready to accept everyone's allegation that it all was a dream, he showed up. He seemed to need to be with me as much as I needed to be with him. Heather was patient and attentive as I told her about my evening. She asked some questions, but never made me feel like I was as crazy as I was beginning to believe.

"My gosh, Sam. To think I was face-to-face with him out there," she said as she tried to absorb my story.

"Hard to believe, isn't it?"

"Well, yes. But even harder to believe that I didn't recognize him at all!" She shook her head.

"You said he had a hat on," I reminded her.

"Yes, but the most famous face in American culture?"

"Yes, well maybe you weren't meant to see." I pointed out. "I don't really know how much power an angel is given really."

My friend still wanted us to go on with our day, desiring to cheer me up. But too much weighed on my mind and my heart to oblige her. I thanked her for her support and promised I'd be in touch with her soon. Heather, always the understanding friend, knew I just needed time alone. We hugged before she left.

As I closed the door behind her, I leaned heavily onto its solid frame. My body felt tired but my mind was very much awake as I scanned the room for signs. I didn't know what I was looking for as I wandered from room to room. I suppose I'd hoped he'd left something of himself behind. My heart sunk as I soon realized there was nothing but memories for me to hold onto. Again.

# CHAPTER 7

The months after that passionate evening passed at a slow, torturous pace. I was distracted relentlessly by my desire to reach out to Elvis and frustrated with my inability to do so.

The airline had assigned me a busy flying schedule, but I didn't mind. My days were filled with bustling airports and hurried passengers who anxiously rushed away to wintry destinations. It was with some dread, however, that I faced the nights. I was always arriving at another hotel in a long list of cities I couldn't even remember. At the end of a flight, I would come to rest my bones once again in a strange bed, but would rarely sleep. Instead, I'd lie awake and wonder if he'd ever come back. I asked myself repeatedly if I was destined to live my life waiting for brief moments with him or should I move on and find true love. In my mind I knew the logical answer, but my heart wouldn't listen. Instead, it hung onto a small glimmer of hope that persistently flickered.

I never told my father about Elvis' last visit. I'd wanted to on many occasion, but always stopped myself. I knew ultimately he would only worry that I was seriously losing my sanity.

The only bright side was that out of this experience had sparked a new, uplifting relationship with my father. For the first time in our lives, we became closer. Though I frequently traveled for work, we made time around my schedule to spend the holiday season together. It was still so strange to not have my mother there, but It was the best Christmas since her passing.

Before I knew it, the New Year had arrived. I joined people in my neighborhood in putting away Christmas ornaments for the season. With winter firmly settled, I wouldn't really see my neighbors again until spring made an attempt. The weather had been anything but pleasant. The wind chill had dipped the temperature to below freezing and gripped the south in its mighty fist.

On one such cold night in January, I crawled into bed with a book to settle in cozy and warm for the evening. After only one page, I became too restless to read, and found myself going over the same lines repeatedly. I put my book down in frustration and propped myself up against my headboard. I wallowed in my boredom as I listened to ol' man winter whistle just outside my window. He sounded angrier every day.

I wondered how long I'd have to wait for sleep to overcome me. My eyes flickered around the room until they rested on my diary. It sat in its abandoned state on the nightstand next to my bed. I thought with little humor that it was funny how this journal haunted me just as much when I was wake as it had in my dream. I picked it up and pondered its significance. My heart filled with the hope I would find entries from my time with Elvis waiting for me inside. I still wished I had something tangible to hold onto. Slowly I opened it and read some of my last entries. Instead of fantasy, I was only faced with the reality of death and sadness. I understood this once-troubled person who had written with such sorrow. With pen in hand, I began to write the next chapter of my life.

*Dear Diary,*

*Or should I say, Dear God? For that is to whom I'm really writing, and to whom I believe now I've always been writing. I used to believe you were not listening, but now know that you always listen and choose when or if to answer. All in your own time and will, as my father would say. This I have accepted.*

*I want to thank you for sending me an angel to help me see my way through the valley. Love is a great gift you have given us, and it's eternal! You can share in it while you walk this Earth, and, as I've learned first-hand, you even experience it long after you've left.*

*Thank you for not giving up on me, though I had given up on you.*

*Love, Sam*
*Your Baby Girl!*

As I closed my diary, my heart felt warm and comforted. Talking to God had made my spirit lighter. I chuckled at the thought of my religious upbringing potentially finally kicking in. I vowed I'd talk with God more often, even if all I had to say was *thanks for the day, see you tomorrow*. I knew He wouldn't always answer me, as children often want or ask for things that possibly aren't in their best interests. But that didn't mean I couldn't ask. As I laid back against my pillow, I closed my eyes in prayer and sent a cosmic question up to the heavens. *Would I see my angel again?* I remained hopeful an answer would come.

With great resolve, I tried to sleep that night. However, Elvis had been on my mind persistently since early that morning. The fact that the next day would have been his birthday didn't help matters. I suddenly felt a longing to go to Memphis. Maybe I would find some comfort in being near the things that meant so much to him in life. As sleep started to take over, I had made up my mind: I would be Memphis-bound come morning.

I packed with an infinite purpose before the break of day. Quickly I moved through my closet and threw whatever looked warm into a small black flowered handbag. I compulsively checked my watch every five minutes, as I was determined to make the first flight headed for Memphis. Not bothering with my own car, I had called a taxi. To my dread, it had arrived quicker then I'd thought and waited outside.

"Sorry, to keep you waiting." I said as I threw my bag inside the back seat of the cab.

"Where to, lady?" Said the driver. He didn't really care what excuse I could offer, he'd heard them all.

"The airport, and I've got a fifty here that says you can make it in ten minutes." I smiled as I waved the bill within the driver's view.

Without a comment, he burned rubber out of my neighborhood. I held on to the door panel and braced myself for the dangerous but necessary pace of the ride. We made it in one piece with exactly one minute to spare.

"Thanks a lot!" I said and gave him the fifty that I'd promised.

I ran into the terminal. My anxiety levels rose as I tried to finish dressing myself while I waited in the security line that led to my gate. I somehow juggled pinning up my hair, taking off my shoes, and digging for my identification.

Once cleared, I ran up to the check-in counter. The gate agent looked at me impatiently as I hopped around trying to put my shoes back on. With only a little scolding about prompt arrival, the agent gave me a boarding pass and asked me to hurry onboard. I ignored the judging looks from fellow passengers who rightly assumed I was the reason they had not left yet. I smiled gleefully and took my middle seat between two of the largest men I'd ever seen. Their arms devoured the armrests on either side of me. I laid back my head and exhaled in relief. I didn't care if one of them fell over and slept on me the whole way to Memphis. I was on my way to see an angel.

* * *

January can be a tough month to visit Memphis. The sun might come out during the day, but then be blocked by gray clouds and snow by evening. Regardless of sun or snow, the one constant was that come nightfall, it was going to be cold. In the past I had always preferred to visit Elvis' gravesite at night. My hope was to have more stamina than the fans that would not want to tolerate the cold temperatures. Such strategy had previously given me some private time in Meditation Gardens, Elvis' final resting place. To visit this time of year was quite different than in August when the summer sun brought hordes of people. While I enjoyed the big, boisterous summer crowds, during the winter I preferred the more tranquil setting of a few quiet groups here and there. I really only needed about an hour, just long enough to walk up to the garden and then back for some much-needed hot chocolate. But I always seemed to linger longer. Once there, I hated to leave.

The night that I arrived was no different than other past winter nights I'd been there—a steady wind blew, and temperatures of around 30° greeted me. Snow had fallen earlier in the day and remained frozen on the ground. On this night of his birthday, fans were allowed to walk up to his gravesite without taking the usual guided tour. Security was positioned along the walk to make sure nobody truly forgot where they were: private property where manners were expected and enforced.

I took my time walking up the famous driveway, a journey that started at the famous Graceland gates. Blue Christmas lights strung along the drive led past a life-like nativity scene and on toward the mansion. Though Christmas had passed, the lights and decorations would traditionally stay up until after his birthday. This was Elvis' wish while he was alive, and it carries on to this day.

Though the cold urged me on as it burned against my face, I still stopped along the way to view the decorations. I was always amazed at the sheer size of the yard ornaments. A large baby Jesus lay in a manger while life-size Mary and Joseph looked on. Even the royalty who bore gifts were in awe of the newborn king.

I continued toward the big house gracefully situated at the top of the hill. Though I learned on my first visit that it was not as big as I'd imagined, it still was of an impressive stature. Large stone lions welcomed visitors up onto a porch that was supported by thick white pillars. The large gated windows commanded attention and always left me with the feeling of being watched.

I stopped at the top of the hill to give the mansion one last look. A security rope drew the line between public and private, but I was close enough to see the detail and admire the architecture. I loved how the small trees that lined the front of the house were decorated with different-colored Christmas lights. The house looked so festive and alive. It was a shame that no one lived within it's walls anymore.

As I approached Meditation Gardens, I could hear the cascading water from the fountain in the garden's center. The sound immediately comforted me. Only a few fans had weathered the cold to find their peace. I especially felt it this visit with the two statues of Jesus present and meaning more to me then ever before. I slowly walked around to Elvis' graveside and noticed someone had tied a single red birthday balloon to the memorial flame. The flame was framed by four glass walls and remained lit year-round. The fiery ornament was a gift from an inner circle of Elvis' friends after his passing. I felt the intensity of the flame and all that it symbolized deep within my heart as I gazed into its glowing embers.

My eyes took in every detail of his bronze grave maker. The color was so deep and rich that I could not read the inscription in the dark of night. Gifts of teddy bears, birthday cards, and flowers were strewn all around his headstone. My heart fluttered lightly. I wondered if he was here watching all this love being showered upon him. I shared in the hope, like other fans, that he was. Soon the last fan left the garden, and I was finally left alone. I peacefully watched the red balloon bounce in the cold winter wind.

"Hello, handsome."

I reached inside my thick coat and gingerly took out a single rose I'd shielded from the elements.

"I brought you something."

I leaned over the small fence that was meant to keep people from walking around the headstone and gently set the flower down with the other tokens of love.

"I didn't want you to think I'd forgotten. I just had to come and say . . ." The words stuck in tightness in my throat. "I miss you."

I took a moment to fight back the tears and fished around in my purse for a tissue.

"But, uh, no more unannounced shower moments, ok?" I laughed while I attempted to regain my composure. "Yes, that seems to be your favorite spot to pop up. I'm now taking more baths than showers, thanks to you."

The cold was beginning to numb me, so I spent just a few more minutes mindlessly watching the birthday balloon bob in the ice-cold breeze. When I thought I couldn't take the temperature anymore, I decided to leave.

"Happy birthday, sweetie. Say hi to my mama for me, would you?"

As I turned to leave I was startled by a male figure that stepped out from the shadows of the night.

"You talkin' to Elvis' grave, luv?"

The stranger was tall and ruggedly handsome. As he stepped closer and into the dim light where I stood, I could make out his short blonde hair and green eyes that were brilliantly visible even in the night.

"Strange, huh?" I said, embarrassed.

"Well, it's a might bit different," he teased in what I guessed was a British accent. "Don't worry, your secret is safe with me."

"Thank you, it's not something I do often. Or, I should say not something I get caught doing often," I tried laughing away the awkwardness.

"My name is Steve. What's yours?" He stuck out his hand for me to take, and I accepted.

"Samantha." I said and lightly shook his hand.

"Your lovely accent tells me you're from around here?"

"Georgia, actually." I said and tugged at my jacket to get warmer.

"Ah, a Southern belle at that," Steve smiled.

My new friend grinned broadly at me. He had a perfect smile. I felt oddly uncomfortable with his flirting, as though the three of us stood there shivering.

"Listen . . . Steve was it? I was just headed to get out of this cold."

"I was considering the same." He said. "Where are you off to?"

I glanced back at Elvis' grave as Steve waited. I started to respond, but then stopped, stunned into silence. The balloon that had been dancing the entire time I'd been there was now as motionless as could be. It stood stock still as if the wind had died, though the hair that tickled my face was proof it had not. In the blink of an eye, it returned to bobbing and straining against the bright red ribbon that held it down. Steve was still talking, though I had no idea what he had said.

My heart skipped happily. Was Elvis trying to send a sign, or was he just a tad jealous? I giggled aloud at the idea of the latter. Well, maybe if he can move balloons he can do other things, like make appearances, if the inspiration hits him.

"You behave, now." I teasingly scolded the balloon.

"Excuse me? You talking to me, luv?"

"Oh, sorry, no. I was just thinking out loud again. You wouldn't be interested in having some hot chocolate with me across the street, would you?" I smiled back at Steve and oozed Southern belle charm.

"That would be great." Steve seemed surprised at my invitation. "Lead the way."

I was elated as we turned and walked away. Despite how cold I was, my step had spring in it. Powerful is women, I thought as I looked back over my shoulder and smiled at the balloon still bouncing with the wind. I felt he was watching as I took Steve's arm into mine.

*See you soon, darlin.*

"Why, Steve, did you say you were married?" I inquired in my best Scarlet O'Hara.

\* \* \*

I walked arm-in-arm out those famous front gates that night with my new friend.

*It's a new day.* A small voice inside my head spoke to my heart as we strolled along in the cold. *Fresh is your soul on this new path.* That promising thought excited me. Though it would take time, I'd come to realize that inspirational thought was not of my own that night. Rather, for the first time in my life, God spoke directly to my heart, just as my father had said he would one day.

I took my first baby steps down the road that leads me to heaven and a promise of eternity. Dare I hope waiting for me is a handsome angel with a song upon his lips? How could I not? After all, it is love that ignites our eternal flames.

# SHORT AUTOBIO

Patricia Garber lives in Washington State with her husband of eighteen years and two loving Labrador retrievers.

Employed by a major airline since she was nineteen, she discovered early that for her travel is not just a job. Rather, it is a passion that has taken her to many exotic destinations. But Memphis, Tennessee remains her favorite corner of the world.

An Elvis fan since she was the age of eight, she has spent thirty years of her life inside the Elvis following that still thrives so long after his passing. Currently, she's the president of the If I Can Dream Elvis Fan Club of Washington State, where the motto is: Yesterday, Today, Tomorrow and Forever.